MAGIC OR MIRAGE

BARBARA CARTLAND

Magic

or

Mirage

DURON BOOKS

MAGIC OR MIRAGE
A Duron Book / 1978

Copyright © 1978 by Barbara Cartland.

Library of Congress Cataloging in Publication Data

Cartland, Barbara, 1902–
Magic or mirage.

I. Title.
PZ3.*C247Mag 1978*   [*PR6005.A765*]   *823′ 9′12*   *78–7964*
ISBN 0–87272–039–X

*Duron Books are published by Brodart, Inc., Williamsport, Pa. Its
trademark, consisting of the words "Duron Books" is registered in the
United States Patent Office and in other countries.*

PRINTED IN THE UNITED STATES OF AMERICA

MAGIC OR MIRAGE

Author's Note

The *Mauretania,* named after Roman Morocco, was, when she was launched in 1907 with her sister ship the *Lusitania,* the largest, most powerful, and fastest oceanliner ever constructed. They took the blue riband of the Atlantic easily and kept it.

The two liners were built with the express idea that they should be convertible in wartime to armed cruisers, but when war was declared in 1914 it was found that the *Mauretania* was too big and consumed enormous quantities of coal. She was laid up.

But after the *Lusitania* was sunk by a German U-boat on May 1, 1915, and 1,198 civilian passengers, mostly American, died, Cunard suspended their Atlantic passenger service and the *Mauretania* became a troop carrier.

After the war, painted a dazzling white, she became a pleasure cruiser. She left New York for the last time on September 26, 1934, to many sad, nostalgic good-byes.

Chapter One

1907

Standing on the steps of the ugly brownstone mansion in Fifth Avenue, Devina sent up a prayer that she might get the job.

She was in fact not over-optimistic about the possibility, but when she had been looking through a newspaper in search of employment, the advertisement had seemed to jump out at her in a manner which she told herself was "meant."

She was getting more and more worried about finding any situation in which she could earn enough dollars to pay for her return fare to England.

It seemed unfair, in fact almost cruel, that her aunt's husband should refuse to give her the necessary money, although for nearly a year she had nursed his wife, run his house, and certainly, if nothing else, saved him the wages of a servant.

But she had known from the moment she arrived in America that he grudged her the food she ate and the fact that she was of the same nationality as his wife.

Samuel Keeward was violently anti-British, and Devina often wondered how her aunt had been brave enough to invite her to come and stay after her parents' death.

The letter had seemed a God-send at the time, when she was feeling desperately depressed and uncer-

1

tain of what she should do about her own future.

There were numerous cousins and one elderly great-aunt with whom she could have made her home, but she knew they did not really want her and had only invited her to live with them out of a sense of duty.

Aunt Louise's letter had seemed to offer her a much more hopeful future, and despite her unhappiness over her mother and father's death she had set out across the Atlantic as if she was an adventurer on a voyage of discovery.

The small drab town in which her aunt lived, the resentment shown by her uncle by marriage, and the hard work she was expected to do were all extremely disillusioning.

But as her aunt's health grew worse Devina had known she could not leave her.

She had in fact put up with innumerable insults to and sneers at the country to which she belonged, simply because, as she told herself, "blood is thicker than water," and because she knew that her aunt clung to her.

Now Aunt Louise had joined her father and mother in Heaven, and once again Devina was on her own. Unfortunately, she was alone in a strange country and without the money to keep herself.

She had refrained from pointing out to Samuel Keeward that she had spent her own money on luxuries for her aunt with which he would not provide her in the last days of her life.

He was an austere man, of evangelical faith, a pillar of his Chapel, who ran a small business with the efficiency of a German General, and she would not lower herself, after the way he treated her, to beg for anything.

He had in fact given her ten dollars, informing her that it would pay her fare to New York and once there she could look for employment.

It had been hard to bite back the many retorts that sprang to her lips and not to inform him, as she longed to do, that her aunt might have lived longer if he had provided her with better doctors.

Devina had told herself she could not bandy words with a man she disliked and despised.

She had come to New York as he had suggested, only to feel bewildered and afraid of the seething city where she knew no-one and had no idea even of where to stay for the night.

Perhaps because she looked extremely pretty but also pathetic and helpless, a kindly Irish-born Policeman directed her to a cheap but respectable Lodging-House where she obtained a minute room for what seemed to her to be an astronomical sum of money.

Then she started to try to find employment.

She thought at first that she would serve in a shop, but she soon found that on most side-entrances there was a notice saying NO HANDS WANTED.

She also learnt that even if she obtained such a position it would take her years to save enough for her fare to England.

She was growing desperate when she saw in the column of a newspaper an advertisement saying:

English Lady of good breeding with high credentials required to accompany young lady to England. Apply 550 Fifth Avenue between the hours of ten and twelve noon.

Devina had only seen the advertisement that morning, having gone out to buy a paper in a drug-store, an American custom which she still found strange.

That she must walk in the streets alone would, she knew, have horrified her mother, but she was careful to walk quickly, keep her head lowered, and not to encounter the eyes of any man who might be looking at her.

Also, as she was dressed in black, the mourning in which she had come from England, she thought that her sombre appearance was not likely to invite those who were in search of gaiety and amusement.

Having read the advertisement, she had hurried back to her lodgings to change into her best straw hat, hoping that she looked older than her nineteen years.

She had the idea that what would be required was a middle-aged or elderly woman, and yet, as she told herself so often, "nothing ventured—nothing gained."

At least she could try to obtain a post which would take her home to safety and security.

As she reached the top of an imposing flight of steps she saw that the front door was open and what seemed an inordinate number of flunkeys with powdered wigs and elaborate gold-braided livery were standing inside the Hall.

A supercilious Butler looked her up and down in a critical manner which was, she thought, almost offensive, before he said:

"I presume you've come in answer to the advertisement?"

"That is correct," Devina replied, "and I would be grateful if you would tell me who inserted it."

She thought for a moment that he would refuse to answer her. Then he said, with a note of surprise at her not knowing to whom the house belonged:

"Mr. Orme Vanderholtz."

"Thank you," Devina said.

The Butler snapped his fingers and she understood that she was to follow a footman across a colossal marble Hall which was lighted by an enormous dome of coloured glass.

An imposing staircase curved up the marble walls and there were two life-size figures of winged goddesses suspended halfway up.

Devina however had little time to notice her surroundings before the footman opened a door and indicated with a gesture of his gloved hand that she was to enter.

It was large, but she realised it was merely an Ante-Room, and seated on a number of claw-footed tapestry chairs were other women, all older than herself and all, she knew, intent on obtaining the post that she desired so ardently.

They looked at her with hostile eyes.

She thought that most of them had been Governesses in their youth, as they resembled the one who had taught her for many years.

She would have liked to chat with them, but she felt they might resent her starting a conversation, and she therefore sat down in an empty chair and looked round her.

The room, she thought, was a cross between a Hotel lobby and an antique-shop.

Sofas covered with Genoese velvet, Oriental rugs, carvings, statuary, and bronzes were everywhere, and there were a number of palms in ancient Chinese bowls that Devina guessed were extremely valuable.

'A lot of money, but not much taste,' she thought to herself.

She thought how her father would have laughed at what was the result of an obvious desire to spend money without any real knowledge of what to buy.

She decided, although she had never heard of him, that Mr. Vanderholtz must be one of the much-publicised American millionaires.

There were, she knew, a great number of them, starting with the Astors, the Vanderbilts, the Goulds, and a great many others.

Samuel Keeward had spoken of them as if they were gods living on a lofty Olympus denied to ordinary human beings.

Devina had been long enough in America to realise that the average American literally worshipped "the golden calf."

They all wanted to get rich quickly, and they all admired and acclaimed those who had already achieved the summit of success.

While Devina was looking round, the door opened and a woman sitting on the chair nearest to it was beckoned by the white-gloved hand of a flunkey.

She hurriedly got to her feet and as she walked from the room Devina suddenly felt sorry for her and for all the others waiting.

There was, she thought, something pathetically eager in all their faces.

She had a longing to talk to them, to ask them

their history, and to learn what they would do if they failed in this instance to obtain the job they required.

She was just plucking up enough courage to speak to the woman nearest to her when the door opened again and another woman was beckoned out in the same manner as before.

'They certainly did not interview her for long,' Devina thought to herself.

She supposed, since the applicants did not return, that they had left by another door, and she was sure she was right in this assumption when only a few minutes later yet another person was called.

Because she was so curious she said to the woman in the next chair:

"Do you know anything about the owners of this house?"

At the sound of her voice every eye in the room turned upon her. Then perhaps because she spoke quietly and gently the woman she had addressed replied:

"Everyone in America knows the Vanderholtzes."

"Except me," Devina said with a smile.

As if her admission of ignorance broke the ice, two or three people seemed to answer at once:

"They are enormously rich, colossally so! They have one daughter and it must be her for whom they need a companion."

"How did Mr. Vanderholtz make his money?" Devina enquired.

"He is a Railway King. You must have heard of him."

"It seems terrible to proclaim my ignorance," Devina answered. "I have of course heard of Mr. Vanderbilt, but never, as far as I can remember, of Mr. Vanderholtz."

"They are both of Dutch origin," one of the women said, "and their families came over to America at least a century ago."

Devina looked interested. Then the woman next to her lowered her voice almost to a whisper as she said:

"It is Mrs. Vanderholtz who is socially ambitious.

She comes from a well-known Virginian family and wants to lead New York Society."

Her informant might have added more but at that moment again the door at the end of the room opened, and one of the women who had been speaking hastily got to her feet, and with a very obvious limp left the room.

"She is not likely to get the job," the woman next to Devina said. "No-one wants to employ someone who is half-crippled."

"Perhaps she has rheumatism," Devina suggested sympathetically.

"You will find in this city that they want those who serve them to be hale and hearty whatever they may be themselves," was the answer.

There were now only three women left in the room besides herself, and they were all, Devina thought, so much older than she was, and due to be interviewed before her, that she decided she had little chance of succeeding where they would fail.

'I might as well leave immediately,' she thought.

Then she thought it was interesting if nothing else to see the inside of a millionaire's Palace.

The hotch-potch of *objets d'art* and antiques which filled the room was doubtless typical of those who left the decorating to those influenced more by desire for ostentation than by good taste.

As if by following the movements of her eyes her companion realised what she was thinking, she said:

"The antique-shops make a fortune in New York. I have often wondered if I could get employment in one of them—at least I know a little more about art than those who compile the appalling mixtures one sees in houses like these."

"If this is typical of other millionaires' houses, there must be ship-loads of antiques crossing the Atlantic from Europe," Devina said.

Her companion laughed.

"There are also a lot of work-shops tucked away in cellars or derelict buildings copying one genuine Louis XIV chair to make dozens exactly like it."

"Is that really true?" Devina asked.

"I assure you that millionaires are tricked and overcharged in every field except that in which they have been expert enough to make their money."

Devina laughed, but she felt somehow as if the whole room disapproved of the sound.

Before she could reply the door opened once again and the woman nearest to it rose.

Even as she did so the footman shook his head and pointed at Devina.

For a moment she thought he must have made a mistake, but when it was obvious that she was required she said hastily:

"These ladies came before me."

The footman did not condescend to reply. He merely beckoned once again, and feeling embarrassed and ashamed of what she thought of as cheating Devina walked across the room.

As she passed the woman who had risen to her feet she smiled at her apologetically, only to receive a hostile stare in return.

Then she found herself in a large Sitting-Room twice the size of the one she had left but which was even more elaborate and packed with treasures.

There was, however, little time to concentrate on anything except the two figures at the far end of the room.

They were seated in velvet arm-chairs and Devina knew as she walked towards them that they were both watching her intently.

She moved gracefully over the heavy carpet, which was so thick that she felt her feet sinking into it as if she walked in sand.

As she reached those who were watching her she made a bow first to the elderly woman, then on the other side of the fireplace to a young girl.

"Sit down!"

The command was sharp and a finger covered in diamond rings indicated a hard, upright chair situated at an exact distance between the two occupied chairs.

"What is your name?"

It was, Devina supposed, Mrs. Vanderholtz who addressed her, and she saw that she was a middle-aged woman who must have been pretty in her youth.

She had aristocratic features and until she spoke might easily have been mistaken for an Englishwoman.

She had both feet on a stool in front of her and her knees were covered with an ermine rug.

She wore, it seemed to Devina, an enormous amount of jewellery—five rows of huge pearls, diamond ear-rings, and a number of narrow bracelets on her left arm.

"My name is Castleton."

"Is that an English name? I've never heard it before."

"It is an old one, as it happens, Ma'am. My family dates back to the fifteenth century."

Mrs. Vanderholtz gave her a sharp glance as if she suspected she was not telling her the truth. Then she said:

"How old are you?"

This was the question Devina had been dreading and she told herself that it was better to return to England by telling a lie than to starve in New York.

"I am twenty-three," she said firmly.

"Tell me about your family."

It was a command, not an invitation.

"My father, who is dead, was Colonel George Castleton and served in the Grenadier Guards. My mother's father was Sir Robert Welwyn of Cheshire."

"You can prove this?"

"I am afraid I have not brought *Debrett's* with me, nor a copy of *Burke's County Families,* but I am sure there would be one in the Public Library from which I could copy the relevant passages."

She thought her reply verged on being impertinent, but Mrs. Vanderholtz accepted it with a sound that seemed like one of approval.

Then for the first time the girl sitting in the chair opposite her spoke.

"She'll do, Momma. Why trouble further?"

Devina, who had been concentrating on Mrs. Vanderholtz, now turned to look at the girl who had spoken and saw that she was very pretty.

There was a resemblance to her mother, and she had fair hair, blue eyes, and a slender figure.

She was extremely well dressed, wore no jewellery, and she had only a slight American accent.

"I have to find out more about Miss Castleton," Mrs. Vanderholtz replied.

"You know everything that is important, Momma," the girl said. "She's English, she's a Lady, and as she has titled relatives she ought to be able to give me all the tips you want me to have before we arrive in England."

"You are too impetuous, Nancy-May, as I have told you often enough before," Mrs. Vanderholtz said, "and in my opinion Miss Castleton is far too young to be a restraining influence upon you."

"Well, if you're thinking of sending me off with any of those harridans we've seen so far, you are much mistaken," Nancy-May said sharply. "They'd drive me crackers before I'd left New York harbour, and I'm quite certain that, for all they may say, they wouldn't know a Duke if they saw one!"

There was silence for a moment. Then as Mrs. Vanderholtz did not speak Nancy-May said to Devina:

"Have you ever met a Duke?"

"Yes, but some years ago," Devina answered.

She was remembering an irate old man who used to come to the Meets to which she accompanied her father and who cursed anyone who got in his way.

"There you are!" Nancy-May said in triumph to her mother. "She knows Dukes, she can tell me about them and that's exactly what you want, Momma."

"It is not as easy as that," Mrs. Vanderholtz replied.

"Look, Momma, you've been going around New York for the past month looking for a suitable Chaperon to travel with me to England. You started off in diplomatic circles, but that was flying too high, and now we are reduced to asking them in off the sidewalks. I say, and I'm the one concerned, that Miss Castleton'll suit me admirably."

Devina held her breath and she knew that Mrs. Vanderholtz was impressed by her daughter's arguments.

"Are you free to travel to England in a week's time as my daughter's companion?" she asked in a voice which made Devina think she would be glad if she was unable to do so.

"I am free now," Devina answered.

It seemed as if this remark gave Mrs. Vanderholtz the respite she was seeking.

"Very well, I will take you on trial," she said. "You will come and stay in the house. I'll instruct you in your duties and if I consider you're not suitable or have not the kind of knowledge I require, then you will leave with a week's wages."

"Thank you, Ma'am. I agree to your suggestion," Devina said with what she hoped was a cool dignity.

"Then let me tell you, Miss Castleton," Mrs. Vanderholtz said, "I shall make every effort to check the truth of what you have told me about yourself, and I shall also watch you to see if your behaviour is in accordance with what I expect from an English Lady."

"I hope I shall not disappoint you, Ma'am," Devina said in a low voice.

"Then you can return to wherever you are staying and collect your trunks," Mrs. Vanderholtz said. "When you return here I will interview you again."

"Thank you, Ma'am."

"Well, thank goodness that's settled!" Nancy-May exclaimed. "And for goodness' sake, Momma, do not bully Miss Castleton so much that she doesn't want to come with me."

"It is you I am thinking of, dear child," Mrs. Vanderholtz said. "If only I could accompany you myself!"

She looked down at her legs raised on the stool as she spoke and sighed.

"You have had an accident, Ma'am?" Devina asked in a sympathetic tone.

"I broke my leg," Mrs. Vanderholtz replied. "As I said to Mr. Vanderholtz, it is criminal that the steps of railway-carriages should be made so high above an ordinary platform."

"It was bad luck, Momma," Nancy-May said, "but you know as well as I do that you were in too much of a hurry. If you'd waited, there would have been half-a-dozen people to help you out."

"You and your father are always unsympathetic!" Mrs. Vanderholtz snapped. "Perhaps you will both listen another time when I criticise the railroads."

As she spoke she rang a small silver bell which stood by her side and when the door opened immediately she said to the footman:

"Order a brougham for Miss Castleton. She wishes to fetch her luggage."

"Very good, Ma'am."

"Thank you," Devina said. "It is very kind of you."

"Do not be too long about it!" Mrs. Vanderholtz snapped. "There is a great deal to be done before my daughter sails at the beginning of next week."

"Yes, Ma'am," Devina agreed.

She bowed to Mrs. Vanderholtz and to Nancy-May, and as she left the room her heart was singing.

She had won! She had gained the position she wanted! She was to go to England!

She could hardly believe it was true until after she had waited only a few minutes in the high domed Hall a brougham came to the front door with a coachman and footman on the box.

As she sat back against the comfortable cushioned seats and a rug was put over her knees, Devina felt she must be dreaming.

She had expected it would take some time to earn enough money for the lowest fare to cross the Atlantic in one of the cheaper ships.

Now she was quite certain she would be travelling deluxe, although that was unimportant beside the fact that she was going home.

The only trouble was that there was no home to

go to, and while at least in her own country she would be amongst relatives and friends, her future was still dark.

*   *   *

Devina joined Nancy-May in what she had learnt was her own private Sitting-Room.

It was slightly less crowded with furniture than the other rooms in the house and was decorated in blue and white, which was supposed to give it a girlish appearance.

However, the carpet in this room also was unnecessarily thick, the curtains festooned with fringes nearly a foot long, the cushions ruched, and there were hot-house flowers stiffly arranged on every side-table.

There was also a magnificent Fragonard on the wall, a collection of delightful Meissen figurines, and the Louis XV furniture doubtless contained priceless examples of the craftsmen of that period.

"What did Momma say to you?" Nancy-May asked as soon as Devina entered the room.

"She told me that I was to teach you to pronounce words in the English fashion, to tell you about the etiquette at English parties, and to keep reminding you to eat your food in the English fashion."

"It might have been worse," Nancy-May said cheerily. "Now sit down and tell me about yourself. We ought to be able to have some fun on the *Mauretania.*"

"Is that the ship on which we will be traveling?" Devina asked excitedly.

She was well aware that the *Mauretania* was the most acclaimed Liner crossing the Atlantic at the present moment.

It had been built to combat the supremacy of the German ships which had snatched the blue riband of the Atlantic from British hands and inevitably cornered the First-Class passenger market.

"Of course we're going on the *Mauretania!*" Nancy-May replied. "Have you not realised by this time that Momma's determined to do everything the English way? I suppose she told you that I'm to marry the Duke of Milnthorpe?"

"Yes, she told me that. You have of course all my best wishes for your happiness."

Nancy-May laughed.

"I can see you're going to say all the right things, and that is what I'm expected to learn from you. What's my future husband like?"

"You have not met him?" Devina asked in astonishment.

Nancy-May shook her head.

"No, and of course I'm not supposed to anticipate that I shall become engaged when I reach England. It is just a formal visit to Milnthorpe Castle."

She gave a little laugh.

"Needless to say, Momma's set the whole thing up. The Duke wants a few million dollars and she wants me to be a Duchess. Easy, isn't it?"

Devina looked at Nancy-May with wide eyes.

"It sounds rather horrid when you put it like that."

"Why not be frank?" Nancy-May asked. "It is the way in which all the other multimillionaires have married off their daughters. Mrs. Vanderbilt nabbed the Duke of Marlborough for hers. Mrs. Goelet caught the Duke of Roxburghe for May, the Duchess of Manchester is an American, and so of course Momma has to have a Duke for me."

"You make it sound so cold-blooded, like a transaction in a shop."

"That is exactly what it is!" Nancy-May said. "But you'll learn that once Momma has set her heart on having something, nothing and no-one'll prevent her from having it!"

"I have heard of the Duke of Milnthorpe," Devina replied, "but I cannot remember why. I know his name often appears in the English newspapers."

"Well, I expect his Castle needs repairing, or he wants to buy some new race-horses," Nancy-May said. "Whatever it may be, Poppa's dollars'll provide it, but he has to take me as well."

Devina smiled.

"I cannot imagine there will be any hardship in that."

"Thank you," Nancy-May said, also smiling. "You wouldn't be so bad-looking yourself if you were not got up in that funereal manner."

"I was in mourning when I came to America," Devina explained, "and now my aunt has died. Quite frankly, I have nothing else to wear."

"Momma will approve!" Nancy-May said. "She likes anyone who serves us to look subdued and unobtrusive. I rather feared she would refuse to have you on the grounds that you were too pretty, but the other applicants were so ugly I suppose she forgot that good looks were supposed to be a disadvantage."

"Why?" Devina asked innocently.

"Because you might be frivolous and attract men, or even rival me!"

Devina laughed unselfconsciously.

"I am quite certain that would be impossible!"

"I hope so," Nancy-May said. "At the same time, once we get on the ship we can enjoy ourselves."

"Is your mother really letting you go alone with me?" Devina enquired in surprise.

"Good Heavens, no!" Nancy-May answered. "I'm to be chaperoned by the British Ambassador's wife, who is returning to Europe unexpectedly because her mother is ill. She's coming here the day after tomorrow to meet Momma, who cannot go anywhere with her broken leg."

"It must be very disappointing for her."

"It is!" Nancy-May agreed. "But by hook or by crook she'll get herself well for the wedding. You can be sure of that!"

"Is it really a secret that you are to marry the Duke?" Devina asked.

Nancy-May laughed.

"It's one of those secrets that everyone knows. You know the sort. They always start by saying: 'You swear you'll not tell anyone . . . ?' "

Devina giggled.

Nancy-May was rather fun and she certainly had a sense of humour.

"You were asking if we're going alone," she went on. "Well, besides the British Ambassador's wife, who, if I know anything, will be a dead bore, we will be escorted by a lady's-maid and two detectives."

"Two detectives?" Devina exclaimed.

"I'm valuable property," Nancy-May answered. "You don't suppose that with my money I'm allowed to go anywhere without being protected? It's been the same ever since I was a child. I've always envied those ragged urchins playing hop-scotch in the street when I drove past with one detective inside the carriage and one on the box."

"Good Heavens!" Devina ejaculated. "I had no idea that heiresses had to put up with that sort of thing!"

"They do!" Nancy-May said briefly. "And doubt-less the Steam-Ship Company'll have Security Men watching me. The stewards and stewardesses'll be vetted in case they snatch a million dollars when they bring in my morning coffee. We'll be lucky if there is not a spy under every bed and every sofa in our State-Rooms."

"It sounds terrifying!" Devina exclaimed. "I think, after all, I am too afraid to be your companion in case you fall overboard and it is all my fault."

"You can't back out now," Nancy-May said quickly. "Think of my being afflicted with one of those aged creatures who would be certain to be horrified at everything I said and everything I wanted to do."

"Poor things! I feel almost guilty at having got the post they wanted."

"You needn't be," Nancy-May replied. "You'll earn every penny, if Momma has anything to do with it! She'll give you lists and lists of instructions, and my advice to you is to burn the lot!"

"I could not be so dishonest," Devina said, but her eyes were twinkling.

She was just about to say something else when a footman appeared at the door.

"Mrs. Vanderholtz wishes to see Miss Castleton immediately!" he announced.

"There, what did I tell you?" Nancy-May asked. "Momma has thought up a few more instructions. Just let them go in one ear and out the other. You may as well get it into your head that I'm going to do what I want."

"I am already quite sure of that!" Devina answered, and heard Nancy-May laugh as she went from the room.

She found however that her newfound employment was far from a sinecure.

For the next seven days she never seemed to have a moment to herself and very little of the time was spent alone in Nancy-May's company.

There were clothes to be fitted, which took up hours every morning, and there were things to be bought, which necessitated exhausting shopping expeditions when they were chaperoned in Mrs. Vanderholtz's absence by one of Nancy-May's elderly relatives.

She was invariably slow and critical, and it took, Devina found, not only hours to buy a pair of gloves but usually resulted in dismantling half the shop before they purchased the pair they had seen first.

Shoe-shops were a nightmare, though it was rather exciting to watch so much money being spent and so much effort put into the adornment of one young woman.

Yet Devina found that by the end of the day she was so tired she fell asleep as soon as her head touched the pillow.

She would have liked to spend a great deal of time in exploring the house, but in the end she found the whole place was like eating too much pâté de foie gras.

The tapestries from France were fantastic and she could have spent a long time following the stories they depicted so skilfully.

But she had to rush to gaze at the Sèvres vases, the statues that had been brought directly from Greece,

the bronzes that had come from Venice and had
originally been cast for a Venetian Prince.

Every country had been combed for treasures;
even the marble with which the house was decorated
had been drawn from old Roman quarries in North
Africa.

Mosaics, porcelains, enamels, Boulle furniture,
Dutch pictures, and Russian ikons jostled each other
in every room.

It was not surprising that the Vanderholtzes employed an army of house-maids and a Housekeeper
who was constantly complaining that the place was
dirty.

At the same time, it was a fascinating glimpse
into a world that Devina had never thought to see.

She knew that when she returned home she would
be able to relate truthfully what life was like in the
houses of the enormously rich Americans.

In the Dining-Room, which could seat a hundred
people without even seeming full, there was silver dis-
played which was worth a fortune in itself and bore
the crests of noble but impoverished families from all
over Europe.

Here Mrs. Vanderholtz entertained nearly every
night, and her parties included not only the elite of
New York but also many of Nancy-May's relatives
who wished to say good-bye to her before she set off
for "foreign parts."

By the way they spoke and the way they looked,
Devina was quite certain they had all been let into the
so-called secret of Nancy-May's visit to England.

Because they were curious they asked her questions which she found not only amusing but often impossible to answer.

"Where does a Duke keep his coronet when he
is not wearing it?" one elderly woman wished to know,
and a man asked:

"Is it true that a Duke's race-horses only drink
champagne?"

At times Devina found it almost heartbreaking
that she could not laugh with her father about the
whole set-up.

It was just the sort of thing that he would have found amusing, and if she had missed him before, she told herself, when she returned to England she would find an emptiness that was almost unbearable because he was no longer there.

At the same time, she had not forgotten that her prayer had been answered.

She had thanked God on her knees beside the heavy, mahogany, canopied bed in which she slept, and when no-one wanted her she took the opportunity to slip across Fifth Avenue and into Saint Patrick's Cathedral.

Devina was not a Catholic, but her mother had always said all religions were good and that if a man could not respect another man's creed, how could he respect his life?

"It is intolerance which takes us into war," Mrs. Castleton said in her soft voice, "and to me the worst intolerance of all is when men will not accept each other's beliefs."

Devina therefore knelt in the incense-fragrant aisle of Saint Patrick's and thanked God for letting her find such an easy way home.

"It might have been very difficult," she said in her heart.

She remembered how afraid she had been of the busy, pulsating city and the fact that she had no-one to turn to for advice.

"Instead, the whole voyage will be an adventure and something to remember for the rest of my life."

She felt as if she was not only speaking to God but also to her father, and she could almost see the twinkle in his eyes and the smile on his lips.

"Whatever I do, Papa," she said, "I want you to be proud of me, just as you were when we were together."

Because she still loved him so intensely she almost expected to feel his arm go round her shoulders and give her a hug.

Then, thinking he must have heard her and knew what she was doing, she left Saint Patrick's Cathedral with a feeling of peace in her heart that had not been there before.

Chapter Two

As Nancy-May had predicted, Mrs. Vanderholtz produced long lists of instructions for Devina before the end of the week.

There were so many items on which she was to instruct Nancy-May, and so many for the American girl to remember, that Devina was quite sure that it was in reality a waste of time.

She had found, however, that Nancy-May was quick-witted and already after being together for a week she was talking with less of an American accent and framing her sentences more in the English fashion.

"Momma's family, whose founder came over from England in the *Mayflower,* always prided themselves on speaking proper English," Nancy-May said when Devina corrected something she said.

Devina thought privately that perhaps during the generations they had been in America their accents had become slightly corrupted by everyone round them.

At the same time, she began to realise as she listened to the guests at luncheon that the well-educated and the well-bred Americans did not speak with a nasal twang which was characteristic of those they called "Yankees."

They were as intelligent, civilised, and interesting as anyone she had met at home, and she knew her father and mother would have liked them.

She was surprised to find how well Nancy-May had been educated.

She had not only had the very best Governesses since her childhood, but also Tutors, experienced in every subject which was considered to be an important part of her curriculum.

Devina was well aware that few English girls would be educated in the same manner.

They were usually dragged up in the School-Room by one inefficient woman, while their brothers were sent to Eton and Oxford, where they assimilated as much learning as they could in the time that was not spent in sport.

She wondered, as she had wondered before, why the English were so indifferent to the education of their women.

She was at times quite envious of all the opportunities Nancy-May had had to learn things in which she personally was interested.

Nevertheless, when the Vanderholtzes were alone, the conversation in 550 Fifth Avenue consisted mostly of speculation about the Duke of Milnthorpe and the importance of making Nancy-May attractive enough to captivate him at first sight.

Mrs. Vanderholtz came from a New England family who, if they had not actually been on the *Mayflower*—it would have had to be a monster ship to hold all who claimed that privilege—arrived in America about that time.

She had been brought up with an elegant, distinguished, and cultured background and had married the Dutch-born Orme Vanderholtz because she fell in love with him.

It was, Devina thought, understandable that her ambition for Nancy-May should be for her to live the same life that she had enjoyed in her girlhood.

This was now unobtainable in America, so Mrs. Vanderholtz looked to the country of her family's origin.

Devina learnt that Mrs. Vanderholtz had made searching enquiries about the British nobility until she found a Duke who was a bachelor.

She further discovered that he was not so wealthy as not to be interested, as many of his contemporaries had been, in acquiring American dollars to keep up his vast estates.

From there Mrs. Vanderholtz had conducted her campaign to ensnare the Duke with the determination and the expertise of a Roman Conqueror.

She was fortunate in that the Duke's mother, the Dowager Duchess, came out to Long Island to stay with the Astors and on meeting Mr. and Mrs. Vanderholtz was as impressed with them as they were with her.

After that everything began to run smoothly.

Mrs. Vanderholtz met the Dowager Duchess again in Paris, where they both had friends amongst the French aristocracy.

By the time Nancy-May had passed her seventeenth birthday the deal was struck and everything was arranged for her to visit England with her mother in April.

"England is delightful at that time of the year," the Dowager Duchess had written, *"and we shall be at the Castle for Easter. I have already invited a small party of friends, and what could be more natural than that our two young people should meet in such congenial circumstances and without our making our intentions for their future too obvious?"*

Nancy-May had shown Devina the letter secretly when her mother was having treatment from the doctors and masseurs who attended her daily.

Reading between the lines, Devina thought that while Mrs. Vanderholtz had told Nancy-May what was intended for her, it was doubtful if the Dowager Duchess had been so frank with her son.

She wondered what would happen if the Duke took an instantaneous dislike to his destined bride. Then she told herself that marriage amongst the leading families in all countries was inevitably an arranged affair.

The bride provided either a vast dowry of money or a great acreage of land, while the bridegroom condescendingly contributed his title.

'It is something I should hate myself!' she thought privately.

Then she laughed at the idea that anything of

the sort was likely to happen where she was concerned.

'I certainly have no dowry to offer anyone,' she thought, smiling, and she wondered if Nancy-May's enormous fortune would ultimately bring her happiness.

She had grown increasingly fond of the American girl by the end of the week.

Nancy-May was not only amusing but full of gaiety and also delightfully unspoilt by her wealth.

This was due to the fact that she had never been allowed to have many companions of her own age and was eternally being lectured and fussed over by her mother.

"I have always wanted what was best for my daughter," Mrs. Vanderholtz had said to Devina when they were alone. "It is not only that she is a very wealthy young woman, but she has a definite personality, which is often lamentably lacking in girls of her age."

That was true, Devina thought, but she wondered whether Nancy-May, having strong opinions of her own, would ever settle down with a man she did not love.

Yet she had been indoctrinated by her mother into believing that an important marriage was the beginning and end of her ambitions.

While it was undoubtedly exciting for her to escape from the luxurious but nevertheless constricting environment in which she had been brought up, Devina sensed there might be many difficulties and heartbreaks ahead.

"At any rate I shall not be there to see them," she told herself.

She had already learnt that as soon as the ship reached Southampton she was to say good-bye to Nancy-May, receive her wages, which she had learnt were to be extremely generous, and take no part in what happened after that.

She had stayed with the Vanderholtzes for almost a week before Mrs. Vanderholtz took any notice of her appearance and was not particularly pleased about it.

She remembered Nancy-May's surprise that her mother had not thought her too attractive to be engaged.

But now there was no doubt that at times Mrs. Vanderholtz looked at her extremely critically and Devina was terrified up to the very last moment that she would change her mind about letting her leave for England with Nancy-May.

She therefore forced herself to be humbly servile in every possible manner and to show Mrs. Vanderholtz that she was carrying out her instructions punctiliously.

"It was a mistake last night," she told Nancy-May, "when your uncle complimented your mother on having found you such a pretty companion. I was terrified that she might dismiss me this morning."

Nancy-May was obviously startled.

"You do not think that could happen?" she asked apprehensively.

"You warned me that your mother did not like her servants attracting too much attention."

"Then for Heaven's sake do something about yourself!" Nancy-May cried. "Pull back your hair and wear glasses! I couldn't bear to lose you now."

Devina smiled.

"That is very nice of you, Nancy-May, and it would break my heart if I could not travel to England with you."

"I'll tell Momma that you've taught me a lot about how to behave in the presence of a Duke," Nancy-May said reflectively, "but I'll also say there is so much to learn still that we shall have to spend three or four hours every day studying."

Devina brightened.

"That is a good idea, especially as I shall be lucky if I can get you to listen to me for five minutes!"

"I'm listening—I'm always listening," Nancy-May protested, "but all I can say is that if the English aristocracy behave as you tell me they do, I would rather marry a rancher and have some freedom."

"You would not find much freedom in having to

do all the cooking and boil your own soap," Devina said with a laugh.

Nancy-May made a grimace.

"No, I guess you're right, but all that etiquette and fuss over who goes in to dinner first'll send me crackers!"

"Mad, or crazy, is a better word," Devina corrected.

"Aw—shucks!" Nancy-May retorted, and the two girls found themselves laughing so much that they forgot to go on worrying.

Nevertheless, it was not until they were actually driving through the City towards the docks that Devina felt safe and on her way home.

It had been, she told herself, a great experience to be with the Vanderholtzes and she was quite certain it would also be an experience to travel to England on the *Mauretania*.

She had come out in a small ship of an American Line operated by a man called Morgan.

He owned a third of the Atlantic passenger trade, and while some of his ships were large and comfortable the others were small and the accommodation was very much the same as Charles Dickens had complained of in 1842.

When Dickens and his wife had crossed the Atlantic for his first American Tour it had been on a Cunard Liner that he described as profoundly uncomfortable.

He had been shown a picture in the Shipping Office of a State-Room. But when he had entered it he had found two berths, one above the other, the upper being an "inaccessible shelf" of which he said: "nothing smaller for sleeping in was ever made except a coffin!"

Devina had remembered his words when on her voyage to America she found that the cabin which she shared with another woman was so cramped that they had to take it in turns to dress and undress.

Now in contrast she was to travel in what Mrs. Vanderholtz informed them smugly was "a floating Palace."

She had been very worried in case Devina let Nancy-May do anything wrong in the eyes of the British Ambassadress, Lady Taylor.

"I have learnt," Mrs. Vanderholtz said, "that the *Mauretania* is the first Atlantic Liner in which it is an invariable rule in the First Class to dress for dinner."

"I will see that Nancy-May does that, Ma'am," Devina murmured.

"And of course she must never walk on deck without you beside her, and you must both of you not only sit with Lady Taylor at mealtimes but also have your deck-chairs beside hers."

Devina nodded.

"Mr. Vanderholtz has been in touch with both the Captain and the Purser, and I am sure you will be well looked after," Mrs. Vanderholtz went on. "At the same time, I realise, Miss Castleton, that you are really too young for this very important and responsible position."

Devina held her breath but Mrs. Vanderholtz continued:

"It is too late to make changes now, but I can say quite frankly that I bitterly regret that Nancy-May overruled me when I was interviewing those who applied in answer to my advertisement. I should have insisted on an older woman."

"I promise you that I will look after Nancy-May and take the greatest care of her," Devina said in all sincerity.

"Mind you do that!" Mrs. Vanderholtz said sharply. "It would be disastrous—yes, disastrous, Miss Castleton—if she should make the acquaintance of undesirable people and the Duke of Milnthorpe should get to hear of it."

She picked up the passenger list which lay on the table before her.

"There are a number of English people on board," she said, "and I have written to Lady Taylor to ask her to make sure that Nancy-May meets only the very cream of Society."

"It only takes seven days to reach Southampton," Devina mentioned, "and I am sure there will be little time for Nancy-May to do anything but acclimatise herself to the sea."

It had in fact been so rough on her voyage out to America that Devina had at times thought that the ship would "turn turtle."

Most of the passengers were far too incapacitated to wish to be friendly with anyone and had lain in their berths, sick and frightened, until they reached the security of harbour.

At any time of the year, Devina had learnt, it was expected that at some stage of the voyage an Atlantic storm should be encountered.

The storms moved round the Atlantic in circles, and one of the officers on the ship in which she had travelled told her that if passengers crossed without seeing a grand and impressive storm they felt they had been defrauded and had paid too much for their passage!

"I personally am a good sailor," Mrs. Vanderholtz was saying with a touch of pride, "but, as Nancy-May has never been to Europe, I have no idea how it will affect her. Mr. Vanderholtz hates the sea and will never board a ship if he can possibly help it, so she may take after him."

"I am sure that as the biggest ship afloat the *Mauretania* will weather any storm," Devina said consolingly.

"It certainly ought to," Mrs. Vanderholtz agreed, but her tone was doubtful.

However, when Devina saw the *Mauretania* moored in the dock it seemed to her so large and so impressive that it would be able to dominate any sea, however tempestuous.

With four funnels it certainly looked, as it had been advertised, "the largest, most powerful, and fastest oceanliner ever constructed."

Mr. Vanderholtz had told Nancy-May the night before they left that it was not only half as big again as any vessel ever built or planned before, but what interested him was that it had three-quarters more power.

"Its engines are steam-turbines," he said. "It is

the first time such engines have been fitted to Express
Liners."

"I can never understand why a ship as heavy as
that does not sink," Nancy-May had said.

Mr. Vanderholtz had instantly gone into a long
and complicated explanation of why such a disaster
was impossible.

Their good-byes to Mrs. Vanderholtz had been,
Devina thought, surprisingly emotional.

She had not detected in the week she had stayed
at 550 Fifth Avenue any particular softness or senti-
mentality about her hostess.

But when she said farewell to her daughter there
was a suspicion of tears in her eyes and a note in her
voice that Devina had not heard before.

"Take good care of yourself, my dearest child,"
she said. "This is the beginning of a new life and I
only wish I could be with you."

"I'll be all right, Momma," Nancy-May had said
confidently. "You look after your leg and get well as
quickly as possible."

"You'll remember everything I've said to you?"

"Everything, Momma! And if I do forget anything,
Miss Castleton'll remind me."

"That's what she's there for," Mrs. Vanderholtz
said, "but I wish . . ."

She broke off her sentence but she eyed Devina
somewhat balefully, as if she resented, despite her
plain black gown, the elegance of her figure and the
pretty face with its big eyes that watched her apprehensively from under a plain travelling-bonnet.

With many last-minute instructions ringing in
their ears, Nancy-May and Devina left the house with
Mr. Vanderholtz.

He was a heavily built, rather ugly man, who,
however, had an indefinable charm which tempered
the strong impression he gave of having an omnipo-
tent, driving power.

The lines on his face and his grey hair told Devina that he had worked hard for his success and
was still fighting to keep the supremacy of his railroads
in his own hands.

She had not had the opportunity of speaking to him except on superficial subjects.

But she had the feeling that, immersed in his battles with those who threatened his Empire, he could be far more interesting than when he uttered the social platitudes that his wife expected of him.

Now he showed his affection for his daughter as, sitting in the carriage, he patted her shoulder and said:

"You have a good time, Nancy-May, and buy anything you want and I'll foot the bill when it comes in."

"Thank you, Poppa."

He made more or less the same speech again when they were shown into the luxurious State-Rooms they were to occupy aboard the *Mauretania*.

There were three of them, Devina found with delight, one decorated in the Adam style for Nancy-May, one in Chippendale designed for herself, and a Sitting-Room between them.

The latter was at the moment a veritable bower from the floral tributes presented to Nancy-May by her father and mother's friends.

There were also huge baskets of exotic fruits decorated with bows of satin ribbon and enough books to read on the voyage to stock a Library.

Mr. Vanderholtz appraised everything, then tipped the stewards in a manner which made Devina feel quite sure that if anyone lacked attention on the voyage it would not be Nancy-May.

Then he sent for the detectives.

They had travelled to the ship in a different carriage with Nancy-May's lady's-maid and a mountainous collection of luggage.

This had all been unpacked before their arrival, and even, Devina found, her own small collection of gowns had been hung up in the wardrobe of her State-Room.

The detectives she had met before, for one or the other of them was always in attendance when they went shopping or was hanging about the passages at 550 Fifth Avenue.

There was an older man called Patrick O'Deary.

The younger was Jake Staten, who was obviously sub-servient and kept well in the background while Mr. Vanderholtz addressed O'Deary.

"One of you are always to keep Miss Vanderholtz in sight whenever she leaves her State-Room, and I've arranged with the Purser that you eat in a corner of the First-Class Dining-Room. I presume that as you were instructed you have evening-clothes?"

"Yes, Sir," Patrick O'Deary replied.

They looked, Devina thought, like ordinary travellers, and it was quite obvious that not only their evening-clothes had come from a good tailor.

"Your cabins are opposite these State-Rooms," Mr. Vanderholtz stated.

Patrick O'Deary nodded.

"We'll take good care of Miss Vanderholtz, Sir. You need not be worried about anything."

"If I am," Mr. Vanderholtz said curtly, "you will suffer for it, and I promise you neither of you will ever be employed in this sort of capacity again."

There was something in the way he spoke which made Devina shiver.

She could understand that a man as powerful and as wealthy as Mr. Vanderholtz could crush anyone who offended him like an insect under his foot.

The detectives were dismissed and Mr. Vanderholtz admonished Nancy-May's lady's-maid to take care of her mistress.

Then as he went into the Sitting-Room Mr. Vanderholtz indicated that he wished to be alone with his daughter.

Without thinking, Devina withdrew not into her own bed-room but into Nancy-May's.

Her maid was putting her gold hair-brushes, which bore her initials entwined on them in diamonds, on the dressing-table.

Devina had in fact been surprised that they had taken with them not the elderly lady's-maid who attended Nancy-May at home but her assistant.

Rose, a Frenchwoman in her early thirties, had spent more time at 550 Fifth Avenue with Mrs. Vanderholtz than with her daughter

"Are you glad to be going to Europe, Rose?" Devina asked now.

"Mais oui, verry glad, *M'mselle,"* Rose answered. "It is five years since I come to New York, an' although I enjoy ze big money one can earn in America I often verry homesick for *la belle* France."

"I am afraid you will not see your own country this trip," Devina said, "unless Miss Vanderholtz pays a visit to Paris on her way home."

The Frenchwoman shrugged her shoulders.

"One never knows, *M'mselle,* an' in England I am nearer France than I am in New York."

This was irrefutable and Devina laughed before she asked:

"Have you been to England before?"

"Non, M'mselle, but I am told English country houses verry uncomfortable an' verry cold in winter."

"I am sure that is true," Devina admitted. "But they can also be cold in America."

She thought as she spoke of how mean Samuel Keeward had been over heating the house because it cost money.

Even when his wife lay ill he had resented the extra expense, and more than once Devina had had to remonstrate with him that her aunt was shivering and that it was undoubtedly worsening her condition.

"There is certainly one law for the rich and one for the poor," she told herself, "but, as Papa would have said, there is no use kicking against it."

She was certainly not prepared to kick or complain against her situation at the moment.

As soon as they boarded the ship she had been tremendously impressed with the manner in which it was decorated and indeed with the good taste shown in everything they saw.

She had already read the brochure issued by the Cunard Company. It described the Grand Staircases as being fashioned on fifteenth-century Italian models and the public rooms as being either French Renaissance or Italian in style.

She looked forward to seeing the Dining-Room, which the brochure described as "straw-coloured oak in the style of Frances I," and which had a dome in cream and gold reminiscent of the Château de Blois.

"I shall inspect everything!" Devina told herself excitedly.

She thought that the comfortable State-Rooms in which she and Nancy-May were to sleep were actually as grand as anything she had seen in 550 Fifth Avenue.

Nancy-May suddenly opened the door of the cabin.

"Poppa wants to say good-bye to you," she told Devina.

"Good-bye, Miss Castleton. I hope you young people'll behave yourselves," Mr. Vanderholtz said heavily. "At the same time, have an enjoyable trip."

"I am sure we will do that," Devina answered. "I have never seen a more marvellous ship!"

"I agree with you and I'm sorry I don't own it myself," Mr. Vanderholtz replied.

Nancy-May gave a cry.

"What a lovely idea! Oh, Poppa, do buy a Shipping Line!"

"It's too late now," Mr. Vanderholtz answered. "It might have been easy five years ago, but now the British with this and its sistership, the *Lusitania*, have scooped the pool."

"Then build one twice as big!" Nancy-May said.

Mr. Vanderholtz shook his head.

"I prefer dry land," he said. "And I've quite enough on my hands to keep me busy for the next year or so."

Nancy-May put her arms round his neck.

"Good-bye, dearest Poppa," she said. "Don't forget me, whatever happens in the future."

Mr. Vanderholtz kissed her cheek.

"I'm not likely to do that," he said, "with your mother nagging me to buy you a tiara to rival the British Crown Jewels!"

"And which would undoubtedly give me a headache," Nancy-May said with a smile.

"That is what many of your mother's propositions give me!" Mr. Vanderholtz replied, and they both laughed.

There were bells ringing to tell all visitors to go ashore.

It had become a custom for the big Liners to sail at midnight from their Hudson River piers.

Devina had heard of the farewell parties that were given on board and that the Liners eased their way out of their berths festooned with paper streamers.

There had been no party for Nancy-May, but on Mr. Vanderholtz's departure they hurried on deck to wave to him standing on the Quay below.

There was a Band playing and the crowd that had come to see them off bombarded the ship with streamers in every colour.

The *Mauretania*'s sirens began to blow the farewell, and Devina, who was musical, realised it was pitched two octaves below middle-A.

There was something very moving in feeling the great ship vibrate under them and the tugs pulling her.

Devina remembered reading somewhere that "the blow from the siren of a ship at midnight carries with it the whole history of departure, longing, and loss."

She and Nancy-May waved until both Mr. Vanderholtz and the pier were out of sight. Then Nancy-May said with a lilt in her voice:

"Now we're really on our way! Aren't you excited?"

"Yes, of course!" Devina answered. "It is the most exciting thing I have ever done."

She looked up as she spoke at the stars overhead, then at the outline of the great buildings of the city still ablaze with lights.

There was, however, a chill wind coming from the sea and Nancy-May shivered.

"Let's go below," she said. "I want to talk to you."

She glanced round as she spoke and Devina realised with surprise that she was looking for the detectives.

There was one of them in the shadows a little

way from them, and Devina saw that Nancy-May made
a sign to him before they moved in through the lighted
door.

She thought to herself it was going to be a considerable nuisance to be followed round the ship by
two detectives, even if the other passengers did not
realise who they were.

She had already learnt in the week she had been
at 550 Fifth Avenue that the detectives were part of
Nancy-May's life and there was no possibility of her
going anywhere without them.

Devina could understand in a way Mr. and Mrs.
Vanderholtz's anxiety when she remembered reading
in the newspapers of the children of millionaires being kidnapped and held for ransom.

Sometimes there were tragic results even when the
money was paid, and the kidnappers in last-minute
panic of being captured had killed their victim.

Nothing of that sort was likely to happen in England, she thought, and decided to tell Nancy-May
that there would be no need for such strict supervision
from her watch-dogs once she arrived at Milnthorpe
Castle.

There were a great number of people congre-
gated in the passages and moving in and out of the
lounges.

Everything was lit so brilliantly that it gave the
place an air of gaiety that was inescapable.

"Do let us look in the lounges before we go
back to our State-Rooms," Devina pleaded. "I am told
that one is like Le Petit Trianon at Versailles."

"All right," Nancy-May agreed good-humouredly,
"but you'll have plenty of time to see everything in the
next seven days."

She had, however, followed Devina into a room
that was beautifully decorated in the French style,
massed with flowers and hung with crystal chandeliers,
and it was extremely impressive.

They also peeped into the Music-Room, which
had a domed ceiling, a carpet in *eau de Nile,* and a
number of sofas and chairs in wild-rose velvet.

"It really is lovely!" Devina said, but realised that Nancy-May was not attending.

"Come on!" she said impatiently. "Let's go back to our Sitting-Room."

There were a great number of other things Devina wanted to see, but she could do nothing but acquiesce.

She opened the door and saw at once that some of the bouquets of flowers had been removed from the sofas and chairs but were still piled in profusion on the tables.

Then as she entered she saw that the younger of the two detectives, Jake Staten, was there before them.

He was standing in the centre of the room and as he smiled at their entrance Devina thought for the first time that he was quite a presentable young man.

Then to her astonishment Nancy-May held out her hand towards him and said:

"At last we've got away! I can hardly believe it!"

"I told you there was nothing to worry about," Jake Staten replied.

They stood hand in hand, and as Devina stared at them wide-eyed, Nancy-May exclaimed:

"Now, Devina, we can tell you everything! Sit down!"

Feeling she must be dreaming, Devina did as she was told. Nancy-May threw herself down on the sofa and drew Jake Staten down beside her.

For a moment they looked into each other's eyes, and as Devina waited apprehensively Nancy-May said:

"This, Devina, is the man I am going to marry!"

Devina gasped.

"What will your ... father and mother ... say?"

"Whatever they say, it'll be too late," Nancy-May replied. "That is, if you will help us."

"H-help you?" Devina stammered.

She was so surprised, so astonished at what was happening, that she felt as if it was difficult to take it in.

She had been indoctrinated in the last six days with the importance of Nancy-May and the fact that she was to be a Duchess!

The plans and arrangements that were made so punctiliously by Mrs. Vanderholtz had superceded everything else and she had hardly noticed Jake Staten or thought of him as a man.

Now she saw that he was in fact not only attractive but intelligent-looking and was obviously completely at ease despite the explosiveness of the situation.

Nancy-May did not answer Devina. Instead she gave a deep sigh.

"You've been brilliant, Jake!" she said. "Absolutely brilliant! I never thought we'd pull it off. Has O'Deary gone ashore?"

"He has!" Jake said with a note of satisfaction in his voice. "And he assured me he was going out West where he belongs and we'll never set eyes on him again."

"He must have been pleased with what you gave him."

"He was delighted! He has wanted to retire for some time and now he can certainly do it in comfort."

"B-but . . . supposing Mr. Vanderholtz finds out what has . . . happened?" Devina interposed.

"How can he," Nancy-May asked, "unless you try to communicate with him?"

Devina looked at her wide-eyed.

"I . . . suppose that is what I . . . should do."

"But you are not going to," Nancy-May said positively, "because I know you are not the type of person to be so disloyal or so sneaky as to ruin my one chance of happiness."

"But . . . somebody will find out before the . . . end of the . . . voyage," Devina stammered.

Nancy-May gave Jake Staten a brilliant smile.

"You tell her exactly how that's not going to happen," she suggested.

Jake Staten bent forward, his eyes on Devina's face.

"It's like this, Miss Castleton," he said. "When I fell in love with Nancy-May and realised she was the one person in the world for me, I had to do some hard thinking."

"Tell her how we fell in love," Nancy-May prompted.

"There was a party," Jake explained, "to which I was invited by the son of the house because I'd been in College with him. His mother doubtless would not have thought me grand enough."

"Tell her what you thought when you saw me," Nancy-May said impatiently.

Jake turned his face to hers.

"I thought you were the loveliest thing I'd ever seen," he answered, "and though I knew it was asking for the moon, I wanted you for myself."

Nancy-May gave a little exclamation of sheer happiness.

"Oh, Jake! And that's what I thought too."

"We only had one waltz together," Jake said to Devina, "but that was enough to tell me that she was everything I dreamed of, everything I didn't believe existed."

"When we said good-night," Nancy-May added, "he said: 'I must see you again! I have to see you!' I had no idea how it could be possible. Momma never let me out of her sight!"

"I hung around Fifth Avenue watching for her and wanting her," Jake went on, "then when I saw she was always accompanied by detectives I knew what I had to do."

"Wasn't he clever, Devina?" Nancy-May asked. "No-one else would have thought of anything half so sharp!"

"But does not Mr. Vanderholtz insist upon employing people with good references?" Devina enquired.

"Of course!" Jake answered. "But I forged those and bribed Patrick O'Deary to say he'd known me for years. It was not difficult once I had him in the bag."

"Jake was so crafty!" Nancy-May said. "When I first saw him come down the passage at home I nearly fainted! Then he wrote me a note and we managed to meet after everyone had gone to bed."

Jake whistled.

"That was a risk I don't want to take again! I thought every moment we'd be discovered and I'd be kicked out of the house before I got my breath."

"We managed to meet a number of times," Nancy-May explained. "Then we knew that we just had to get married, and that stuck-up English Duke can just go and jump at himself as far as I'm concerned!"

"Wh-what will your . . . mother say?" Devina asked anxiously.

"What can she say once I'm Mrs. Staten and belong to Jake?"

Devina could imagine Mrs. Vanderholtz's anger at what had occurred but aloud she said:

"Suppose the . . . Press get to hear of it before you are actually . . . married? They may find you out when you reach England."

Nancy-May looked at Jake again and they both laughed.

"You're underestimating the wonderful man I love," Nancy-May said. "Tell her, Jake, what we intend to do."

"We're going to be married in Scotland, where it's far easier than in any other country," Jake said. "We thought of France, but when I went into details it seemed a bit dicey. Scotland's ideal, but you'll have to give us time to get there."

"Me?" Devina asked.

"Yes—you!" he said firmly. "As you've so rightly said, our real enemy at the moment is the Press."

Devina could not think of anything to say. She could only wait.

"Needless to say, there are reporters on board," Jake went on, "who know that Miss Vanderholtz is travelling to England and that she's of marriageable age. They'll be after every tit-bit of information they can get."

"That is what . . . I thought," Devina murmured.

She had been well aware while she was in New York that the Press was always trying to get information about the Vanderholtzes, as they were about all the other important families belonging to the much-vaunted Four Hundred.

She had seen reporters waiting on the steps when they went driving and she was sure they continually bombarded the servants with questions.

Mrs. Vanderholtz had spoken scathingly of the scurrilous newspapers that were published in New York and the interest they showed in Nancy-May.

"We'll give them the coverage they want when the engagement is finally announced," she said to Devina. "In the meantime I'm only praying they'll not get a hint of where Nancy-May'll be staying in England."

Now Devina gave a sigh as she said:

"If there are reporters on board they will certainly try to interview you."

"That's true," Jake agreed, "and it would be pretty hard to stall them off for seven days. That's why we have to act quickly."

"Tell her, Jake! Tell her what she has to do," Nancy-May prompted.

"It's quite easy," Jake said. "You have to be Nancy-May until we are married!"

For a moment Devina could not take in what he was saying. Then she gave a little gasp.

"Be Nancy-May?" she repeated. "B-but . . . how? What are you . . . suggesting I do?"

Jake smiled.

"The only person at the moment who knows what you both look like," he said, "is Rose. Well, I've fixed her. The one thing she wants is to get back to Paris."

Devina's eyes were wide with astonishment as he went on:

"She'll not breathe a word. The stewardesses have not seen you and actually, as I expect you realise, you and Nancy-May are rather alike."

"That is why I chose you," Nancy-May cried. "Now you understand why I wouldn't have any of those awful old women that Momma thought were the right age for a companion."

It had not struck Devina before that there was a resemblance.

Yet as it happened she and Nancy-May were the same height and of similar build. They both had fair hair and their eyes were their most predominant feature.

Nancy-May's were blue and hers were greeny-grey, her skin was undeniably whiter than the American girl's, and her mouth was fuller.

But to a casual glance there was not a great deal of difference between them and Devina thought that if she were dressed in expensive clothes anyone who did not know Nancy-May intimately might easily be confused.

"What you have to do," Nancy-May said as Devina did not speak, "is to move into my State-Room and behave exactly as if you were me. I shall sleep in yours, but I warn you I refuse to wear those black funereal clothes. I want to look attractive for Jake."

"You always look attractive to me," Jake said softly, "whatever you wear."

For a moment they were too preoccupied with each other to remember their problem and Devina recalled them to the vital subject at hand as she said:

"You have forgotten one person."

"Who is that?"

"Lady Taylor!"

Nancy-May gave a little whoop of delight.

"It's not we who have forgotten—it's you! Lady Taylor has never seen me."

"That's right!" Devina exclaimed. "You had a terrible headache the day she came for luncheon and had to lie down in a darkened room."

She paused to ask:

"Was that . . . an act?"

"I've always thought I ought to have been an actress!" Nancy-May laughed.

"Well, you certainly deceived me!" Devina said.

"Let's see if we can manage to deceive everybody else." Nancy-May smiled. "I've been training myself to remember that I'm Devina Castleton, a well-behaved, well-brought-up English girl."

"You may be able to act the part of an English girl," Devina retorted, "but I am never going to get away with being American!"

"Why not?" Jake enquired. "You've only to add

an American accent to some of the words you say, and Nancy-May's now speaking such good English she sounds like a foreigner half the time."

He was teasing and Devina had to laugh.

"I cannot do this!" she said at length. "It seems so . . . wrong . . . so disloyal to your father and . . . mother."

"Your loyalty is to me," Nancy-May said firmly. "You know as well as I do that Momma would never have engaged you if I hadn't insisted. I'd even threatened her before you came in that if I had to go to Europe with one of those ghastly old women I'd refuse to go at all!"

She smiled before she added:

"I was just praying somebody young had applied and when you appeared I knew it was fate."

Devina remembered how she thought it was 'meant' that she should see the advertisement in the newspaper, and it had certainly been a beneficial paper as far as she was concerned. Why then should she try to deny Nancy-May her happiness?

She knew they were waiting for her to speak and after a moment she said:

"I will . . . do it . . . but I warn you I may let you . . . down, and quite frankly I am . . . terrified!"

Nancy-May jumped up from the sofa and kissed her.

"You're a honey!" she said. "Make no mistake, with Jake as Stage Manager we'll all put on such a magnificent performance that no-one'll guess for one moment that we're not who we appear to be."

"It is . . . a risk!" Devina said feebly, feeling as if she were being swept along by a tidal wave.

"What are risks for except to be enjoyed?" Nancy-May asked lightly, "and this, dearest Devina, I assure you is going to be the most enjoyable, most fabulous journey we've ever dreamt about!"

Chapter Three

Devina came back to consciousness as a voice said:

"You sure look pretty in the morning!"

"You *do* look pretty!" she murmured and opened her eyes.

Nancy-May was sitting beside her on the bed, wearing a lace-trimmed negligé, her fair hair hung over her shoulders.

"I thought you were Mrs. Rip Van Winkle," she teased, and Devina sat up, wiping the sleep from her eyes.

"I stayed awake very late," she excused herself, "worrying about you."

"There's no need to do that," Nancy-May replied.

Devina hesitated before she said in a very low voice:

"Nancy-May, you are quite, quite certain that you love Jake and he really loves you for . . . yourself?"

"You're behaving just like Poppa and Momma," Nancy-May retorted petulantly.

"They would be worried, as I am, simply because they love you," Devina said. "After all, you are sensible enough to know that your being so very rich is bound to be an attraction to some sort of men."

"Jake's not like that," Nancy-May answered. "He

42

loves me for myself. We told you we both fell in love the moment we met each other."

Again Devina hesitated before she answered:

"Yes, I know, but you have not seen many men in your life, Nancy-May, and you certainly have not had them making love to you."

Nancy-May gave a little sigh of happiness.

"It's so exciting and so wonderful to have a man telling me how much he wants me and how I'm everything he looked for all over the world and couldn't find."

Devina did not speak and she went on:

"Jake says I'm different—different from any woman he's ever met—and he's planning all the marvellous things we'll do together once we are married."

Devina resisted an impulse to ask who would be paying and knew she was being cynical and perhaps over suspicious, but she could not help feeling that Nancy-May had jumped at the idea of marrying Jake far too quickly.

It was, she thought, inevitable that she should be excited and thrilled by her first love-affair, but that did not say that Jake was a suitable person for a husband or that eventually she would be happy with him.

And yet, she asked herself, was the alternative very satisfactory?

No girl, however socially ambitious, could really want to marry a man she had never seen and about whom she knew nothing except that he was a Duke.

Before she went to sleep she had gone over and over the position in which she found herself.

She felt she was being disloyal to the Vanderholtzes, who paid her wages. At the same time, she could not face the thought of betraying Nancy-May and getting in touch with her father and mother to prevent her marriage.

"Perhaps I shall feel more reassured by the whole idea before we reach England," Devina had told herself before she went to sleep.

Now she saw that Nancy-May was looking at her

with an apprehensive expression in her eyes as she asked:

"You're not going to do the dirty on me, Devina?"

"I have considered it," Devina answered frankly, "but supposing I interfere and then you are unhappy for the rest of your life?"

"That's exactly what I shall be if I cannot marry Jake," Nancy-May said. "You must see how irresistibly attractive he is, and when you know him better I'm sure you will find, as I have, that he has a strong character and a determination that will take him to the top."

Nancy-May spoke with an almost ecstatic note in her voice and again Devina could not help thinking cynically that it would be fairly easy for Jake to get to the top if he had Nancy-May's money to assist him.

Instead she said:

"The ship is rolling a little."

"The stewardess said we should be running into a storm before noon," Nancy-May replied.

"The stewardess?" Devina questioned.

"I rang for her," Nancy-May explained, "and I said to her: 'I'm Miss Castleton, and I understand you're looking after Miss Vanderholtz and myself. I don't think she is awake yet, so perhaps you'll arrange for the breakfast to be brought into the Sitting-Room.' "

Nancy-May had spoken slowly and in a manner which showed that Devina's teaching of good English had been effective.

Devina clapped her hands.

"That was good, Nancy-May, very good!"

"I thought you'd think so!" Nancy-May laughed. "Now you'll understand why I listened so attentively to you."

She rose from the bed to walk across to the dressing-table.

"There's no reason why anyone should question the fact that I am English," she said. "Momma had a very square chin as a girl, which might have been a

give-away, for I believe most English people have slop-
ing chins, if they have one at all!"

"That is an insult!" Devina laughed. "But I will
admit that your face is not predominately American,
and if you will remember not to speak through your
nose and distort your words you may pass in a crowd."

Nancy-May laughed and picking up a lace-
trimmed cushion threw it at her.

There was a knock on the door.

"Breakfast's ready, Miss Vanderholtz," a voice
said.

There was only a slight pause before Devina answered:

"Thank you."

Both she and Nancy-May waited until they heard
the Sitting-Room door close, then Nancy-May said
excitedly:

"Now that it's established who we both are, you
can't back out."

"I ought to," Devina said seriously.

"But you'll not, and that's all that matters."

By the time they had finished breakfast the ship
was rolling quite considerably.

"There's really little point in dressing," Nancy-
May said. "I may have to lie down if I feel sea-sick."

"If you want to talk to Jake you will have to
dress," Devina said quietly.

"Yes, of course," Nancy-May agreed, as if she had
forgotten about Jake, "but I hope you'll spare me
Rose."

By the time the two girls were dressed the movement of the ship was very noticeable, but Devina, who
had been in a much worse sea, was not in the least
perturbed.

Nancy-May was apprehensive that she might be
sea-sick, but then she started to talk animatedly about
herself, and when Jake came to the cabin she forgot
everything but what lay ahead.

Devina found that this was her opportunity to
examine Jake critically.

There was no doubt that he was prepossessing,

but she did not know enough about Americans to be able to decide as she could have done in England what was his background or if he was what most people would call a "gentleman."

'It was obvious that Nancy-May was desperately in love with him, and he certainly was very loving towards her.

He paid her compliments, speaking very affectionately, and looking into her eyes in a manner which made it seem as if everything they were about to say had gone out of their heads.

After they had talked for a little while of their marriage and how they could contrive to get to Scotland by the quickest possible means, Devina said tactfully:

"I think I will go to my own room and read."

"Don't do that," Jake said. "I'm going to take Nancy-May up on deck. She's much less likely to be sick if she's out in the fresh air."

"I don't feel sick yet," Nancy-May said, "but I would love to go with you."

"Then wrap yourself up," he said. "I don't suppose there will be many people about to see you, and if they do, why should not Miss Vanderholtz's companion take a turn on the deck with Miss Vanderholtz's detective?"

"Why not indeed?" Nancy-May replied.

She hurried into Devina's State-Room to find a coat to wear and a chiffon veil to put over her hat to keep it from blowing away.

By the time Devina had helped dress Nancy-May she thought it was very unlikely that anyone looking at her closely would imagine she was the heiress to the Vanderholtz millions.

They found a plain brown chiffon veil which covered her hat and tied it in a bow under her chin, and her pretty gown had disappeared under a heavy tweed coat.

Mrs. Vanderholtz had insisted Nancy-May should take this with her in case it was cold and wet.

"I've always hated that colour!" Nancy-May said petulantly. "It makes my skin look sallow."

"All the better if you do not look too pretty," Devina said with a smile.

"But I want to look pretty for Jake. Think how ghastly it would be if he thought you were prettier than I!"

"There is no possibility of that," Devina answered.

Once again she worried as to whether Jake was in love with Nancy-May herself or with her untold millions.

"We'll not be long," Nancy-May said when they joined Jake in the Sitting-Room.

"Be careful not to get washed overboard," Devina admonished.

"I'll take care of that," Jake answered.

When they had gone Devina inspected the books that had been sent as farewell gifts and found that she wanted to read nearly all of them.

She had a suspicion that they had been chosen because they had just been published and had received effusive reviews from the critics, rather than because they were to Nancy-May's taste.

She decided to read first a book on Egypt, and had settled herself comfortably on the sofa with her feet up when there came her first interruption.

It was the steward with a note for Miss Vanderholtz.

Devina opened it to find it was from Lady Taylor.

She wrote most pleasantly, saying she deeply regretted she had not been able to meet her charge last night, but she had come on board rather late after being kept at a Reception at the Embassy.

She however hoped that she would be able to make Miss Vanderholtz's acquaintance later in the day, although at the moment, being a very bad sailor, she was unable to leave her cabin.

Devina read what was written, then said to the steward:

"Will you thank Her Ladyship and say I hope she will soon feel better?"

The steward smiled.

"That's unlikely, Miss. We've not met the full force of the gale yet."

"Are we running into one?" Devina enquired.

"That's what we've been told, Miss. And if you takes my advice you'll have your luncheon in here. There won't be many of them as'll stagger down to the Saloon, unless the wind drops."

"I think that is a good idea," Devina said. "I will ask . . ."

She stopped.

She had just been about to say: "I will ask Miss Vanderholtz," then remembered it was for her to give orders.

"Yes," she said firmly, "please bring luncheon here at one o'clock."

"Very good, Miss. I'll bring the menu a bit before and you can choose what you'd like to eat."

"That would be very nice, thank you."

The steward left and Devina settled down once again to her book.

Rose had already retired to her cabin, looking green, and Devina thought it was unlikely that she would be very much help until the storm was over.

She had decided it would in fact be best if, as Miss Vanderholtz, she was seen as little as possible in public.

If, as Jake said, there were reporters on board, then there was always the chance there might be one who had seen Nancy-May often in New York and would think perhaps she had changed.

There were so many hazards in carrying out a masquerade of this sort that Devina found it almost impossible to concentrate on her book.

She worried about what seemed in retrospect an undertaking on behalf of Nancy-May and Jake Staten that was both crazy and reprehensible on her own part.

"What can I do?" she asked herself. "How can I refuse them or justify my action to the Vanderholtzes?"

For a moment she felt frightened of being involved in something which undoubtedly would eventually cause a great scandal, unless the Vanderholtzes took the wise course of keeping everything quiet.

But would that be possible?

Devina did not know the answer, and at the moment she felt that the only thing she wanted to do was run away, hide, and just be herself.

But that was quite impossible, at any rate for the next seven days.

They were at sea, and she knew that even if at this late hour she tried to take a stand and refuse to go on with this pretence, it would be impossible.

How could she resist the pleadings of Nancy-May and Jake, or, worse still, evoke their anger?

'I do not think anything really matters until we reach Southampton,' Devina thought. 'But how then can I go to Milnthorpe Castle and meet the Duke, when he will think that I am Nancy-May?'

Just as it had done last night the whole plot went round and round in her head, and yet she could find no escape.

'Perhaps they will change their minds by the time we reach England,' she thought optimistically, but felt her hopes would not be realised.

Determinedly she concentrated once again on her book, and, just as before, there was a knock on the door.

"Come in!" she called, expecting it to be the steward.

The door opened and a gentleman stepped into the cabin.

He was tall, square-shouldered, and had a sunburnt face. It flashed through Devina's mind that he might be a reporter and she should not have been so careless as to let him in.

"Who are . . . you and what do you . . . want?" she enquired.

There was an obvious nervousness about the question, which brought a smile to the face of the man who was advancing towards her a little unsteadily owing to the movement of the ship.

"Perhaps," he replied, "it would have been more correct for me to have asked the steward to announce me. My name is Galvin Thorpe and I am anxious to make your acquaintance."

Devina did not speak and he went on:

"That is, if you are in a fit state to receive anyone, which in fact I can see you are."

He reached the sofa on which Devina was lying and put out his hand. Because there seemed to be nothing else she could do, Devina put out hers.

He shook it and said:

"I hope you do not mind if I sit down?"

"N-no," Devina said, "but if you are a reporter I think I should . . ."

"I have already told you—my name is Galvin Thorpe," the newcomer interrupted. "You will be staying with my first cousin when you reach England."

Devina felt her heart give a little jump of fear.

"How stupid of me . . . of course!"

He bore the family name of the Duke of Milnthorpe and she should have remembered it.

Hastily, in order to cover what she felt was a slip on her part, she said:

"I am sorry. I did not know you would be aboard."

"Of course not," Galvin Thorpe agreed. "I did not know it myself until I reached New York yesterday afternoon and saw no reason not to return home on the most comfortable ship afloat."

"You have been staying in America?" Devina asked politely.

She was wondering frantically what she should do in this unexpected situation, and she knew that the only thing possible was to try to behave naturally, without showing how nervous she was.

"As it happens, I have been in Alaska," Galvin Thorpe said.

"How . . . how interesting," Devina murmured. "But it must have been very . . . cold."

"Extremely!" Galvin Thorpe agreed. "And it was, I may say, a very great change from Africa, where I had been previously."

Devina looked at him wide-eyed and he explained:

"I am what is commonly known as an explorer, and as I am writing a book I thought the extremes of two Continents might make an interesting comparison."

"Very interesting indeed!" Devina agreed.

She had the uncomfortable feeling that Galvin Thorpe was looking at her searchingly, in a manner that made her also feel afraid.

"How . . . how did you know I was going to . . . stay at Milnthorpe Castle?" she asked.

She felt it was important to learn his explanation and thought that the searching look in Mr. Thorpe's eyes was intensified as he replied:

"When I went to the Travellers' Club in New York to have luncheon, quite a number of people I knew informed me that you were to marry my cousin."

Devina started.

She had not expected him to say anything so blunt.

She could not meet his eyes and instead looked down at her lap.

"It is . . . just a . . . visit," she said hesitatingly, "arranged between the Dowager Duchess . . . and my . . . m-mother."

It was difficult to speak of Mrs. Vanderholtz in such a familiar way.

"That I might have guessed," Galvin Thorpe said. "My aunt is a very managing person. But I understand your mother is not with you."

"No . . . unfortunately, she broke her leg last month."

"And so you are setting out for England alone?" Galvin Thorpe asked with a touch of surprise in his voice.

"I have a . . . companion with me, and I am being . . . chaperoned by the British Ambassadress, Lady Taylor."

"That sounds very respectable," he said. "Now tell me—are you looking forward to meeting your future husband?"

The way he spoke made Devina angry.

"I think I should . . . point out, Mr. Thorpe," she said in what she hoped was a crushing tone, "that if

you have listened to a lot of ill-informed gossip I do
not think you should repeat it to me."

She thought Galvin Thorpe looked surprised. Then
after a moment he said:

"If I have done anything to offend you, Miss Vanderholtz, I must apologise, but I was informed cate-
gorically and without a shadow of a doubt that the
marriage was already arranged."

"I have not yet . . . met your cousin . . . the
Duke," Devina said coldly.

"And he has not met you," Galvin Thorpe said,
"so of course I must reserve my congratulations."

She did not speak but just bowed her head.

There was a somewhat uncomfortable silence before Galvin Thorpe rose to his feet.

"I think you would wish to continue reading
your book, so I will bring my courtesy call to an end,"
he said. "If there is anything I can do to help you on
the voyage, I hope you will feel free to ask me."

"Thank you," Devina answered, "but I am sure
everything possible has been done to make me comfortable."

She looked at him as she spoke and realised that
there was some sort of war between them.

She had a feeling that there was a look of contempt in his eyes and she was sure it was because he
had not been in the least deceived by her prevarication
about the engagement.

He knew as well as she did that the arrangements
between the Dowager Duchess and Mrs. Vanderholtz
would end in the Duke of Milnthorpe coming into
possession of Nancy-May's millions and Nancy-May
becoming a Duchess.

'He is shocked at the idea,' Devina thought to
herself, and she could hardly blame him.

At the same time, there was no need for him to
have been quite so abrupt and overbearing about it.

Now she said:

"Good-bye, Mr. Thorpe, and thank you for calling
on me."

She spoke in a proud manner that her grandmother, who had been a very awe-inspiring old lady, might have used.

"Good-bye, Miss Vanderholtz," Mr. Thorpe replied. "I expect we shall meet at luncheon or dinner. I am also at the Captain's table."

Devina did not reply. She merely watched him as he crossed the cabin and opened the door.

Then as he did so she heard Nancy-May's vivacious voice outside in the corridor. She must have bumped into Mr. Thorpe as he left the cabin, for Devina heard her say:

"Hello! Who are you?"

"My name is Galvin Thorpe and I have just had the pleasure of calling on Miss Vanderholtz," Mr. Thorpe replied. "I imagine you must be Miss Castleton?"

'He is certainly well informed,' Devina thought to herself.

Then she knew it would be quite easy to find out from the passenger list or the Purser who was travelling in the entourage of Miss Vanderholtz.

"That's right, I'm Miss Vanderholtz's companion," she heard Nancy-May say in a quieter tone than she had used before.

There was a little pause and Devina had the uncomfortable feeling that Mr. Thorpe was looking at the man who accompanied her.

Without saying a word he must have communicated his curiosity to Nancy-May, for she said:

"This is Mr. Jake Staten, who is looking after Miss Vanderholtz on the journey."

"A detective!" Mr. Thorpe exclaimed.

"Exactly!" Jake answered him. "And a very good one, in case you're interested."

He spoke aggressively and Devina drew in her breath.

Like her, Jake did not know or had not guessed who Galvin Thorpe was likely to be.

"I am sure that is very necessary where Miss Vanderholtz is concerned," Galvin Thorpe said.

He must have turned and walked away, for Nancy-

May, followed by Jake, came hurrying into the cabin.

"Who was that? What was he doing here?" Nancy-May asked, while Jake Staten, having shut the cabin door, said angrily:

"Why do you want to entertain strangers who might be dangerous?"

"I did not mean to entertain him," Devina said. "He just walked in and introduced himself."

"Why should he do that?"

There was something almost offensive in the manner in which Jake asked the question.

"He happens," Devina answered slowly, "to be the first cousin of the Duke of Milnthorpe!"

There was a startled silence. Then Nancy-May, throwing herself down in a chair, exclaimed:

"That's torn it! Why were you so rude to him, Jake?"

"How was I to know who he was?" Jake asked. "I thought he was some know-all connected with the ship, or else a reporter!"

"Well, he's not, he's a cousin of the Duke, and if he should be suspicious . . ."

Nancy-May stopped speaking and her eyes were suddenly very wide and apprehensive.

"Oh, Jake! Supposing he telegraphs Momma for an explanation?"

"Now calm down," Jake replied. "Why should he do anything of the sort? He thought you were Miss Castleton, and there's no reason why a companion shouldn't be walking about with me, and being friendly, if it comes to that."

Nancy-May gave a quick sigh.

"No, of course not. I'd forgotten."

"What did he say to you?" Jake asked Devina.

"He came to call on Miss Vanderholtz," she replied, "because he had heard at his Club in New York that she was to marry his cousin!"

"It's supposed to be a secret!" Nancy-May cried.

"Of course it's not a secret," Jake Staten said. "How could you keep it a secret with your mother shouting the good news from the housetops?"

Nancy-May was looking at Devina.

"Do you think he was suspicious?" she asked.

Devina shook her head.

"No, I am sure he was not. He was just rather hostile! I do not think he . . . wants you to . . . marry his cousin."

"Then that's a good thing," Nancy-May said quickly, "because I'm not going to!"

"You're going to marry me," Jake said, "and don't you forget it for one moment!"

"Am I likely to?" Nancy-May asked. "I'm only afraid, desperately afraid, that something'll stop us."

"Nothing'll stop us if we're clever about it," Jake said, "but I don't like the sound of this Thorpe fellow."

"He is an explorer," Devina explained, "and he only arrived yesterday in New York from Alaska. It is just bad luck that he chose to sail on this ship."

"That's the truth," Jake agreed. "Just bad luck."

There was silence for a moment. Then Jake said as if he was trying to control the situation:

"We've just got to be on our guard. It was stupid, I see that now, to come laughing and talking down the corridor. But it would be quite a natural thing for Miss Castleton to do as she's only a companion."

Devina did not contradict him, but she thought that it would in fact have been very unnatural.

In the Vanderholtz house in Fifth Avenue the detectives had been treated as if they were servants. They were given orders and otherwise ignored.

They were always watching over Nancy-May, but there was no question of her conversing with them when they travelled with her in the same carriage or talking to them in the house except to say good-morning or good-night.

Patrick O'Deary had in fact been of the same class as the coachman or the gardener whom her father had employed in the past.

Only Jake was different in that he was obviously educated and had, if he was to be believed, moved in social circles.

He got up now to walk restlessly across the cabin.

"There's no blood spilt so far," he said. "All

we have to do is be more careful in the future."

He put his hands on the back of the sofa on which Devina was lying, and bending over her said:

"And don't you encourage him!"

"I have no intention of doing so," Devina answered, "but it would certainly not be good policy to be rude to one of the Duke's relatives."

"No, of course not," Nancy-May agreed. "Devina's right, Jake. If anything, we have to be extra nice to him, otherwise he may make trouble before you and I can reach Scotland."

"Mr. Thorpe told me he was sitting at the Captain's table, as we are," Devina said, "but I have ordered luncheon in here for us today."

"Why did you do that?" Nancy-May asked.

The way she spoke told Devina that she thought she was presuming on her authority.

"The steward suggested it," Devina explained. "He said as it would be very rough, few people would go to the Dining-Saloon and he thought we would be more comfortable here."

"Yes, of course we should," Nancy-May replied in a different voice. "It was very sensible of you to do what the steward suggested, wasn't it, Jake?"

He did not reply and after a moment she went on:

"I've just realised that if we have luncheon here, you can have it with us."

Devina was about to say that it was an unwise thing to do, then she told herself it was none of her business.

She was well aware that the part she had to play was not going to be very easy.

There already seemed to be undercurrents in everything they said to each other, and she also had the impression that if anything went wrong Jake might be nasty about it.

She gave a little sigh and wished with all her heart that they were just taking the voyage in the ordinary way as she had imagined they would when they first came aboard.

Instead of which, already they were mixed up in a terrible tangle.

"Are you worried, Devina?" Nancy-May asked.

"Yes," she admitted, "and if I am honest, Mr. Thorpe rather frightened me."

"There's no call for you to be afraid," Jake said. "After all, if he's a relative he's not going to kick against all those lovely dollars that he imagines Nancy-May will be pouring into the family exchequer."

Devina did not answer. Although there was no reason why she should think so, she felt that Mr. Thorpe was not particularly interested in money.

*　　*　　*

During the next two days the *Mauretania* passed through a very bad storm and Devina was thankful she was not travelling in the small, uncomfortable ship in which she had reached New York the previous year.

It might not have sunk, but she was certain that a number of people would have broken their arms or legs.

As it was, the *Mauretania* sailed almost serenely through a tempestuous sea, and, although the steward informed them that most passengers kept to their cabins, neither Devina nor Nancy-May felt in the least sea-sick.

There were, however, very few passengers brave enough to venture out to the wet decks. When finally Devina achieved it and felt the wind whipping her cheeks and blowing in her face, it gave her a sense of exhilaration after being confined.

She and Nancy-May were of course accompanied by Jake, and he found them a place to shelter against the superstructure where they could see the green sea breaking over the bow.

It was a fascinating sight, especially as the sun came through the grey clouds above and turned the sea to every conceivable colour.

Nancy-May shivered.

"I do hope we're not going to be ship-wrecked.

Can you imagine what it'd be like trying to swim in waves as big as those?"

"You would not be trying for long," Devina said. "When I thought the ship in which I came out from England would founder, it was my one consolation that death would come very quickly."

"That's morbid!" Nancy-May explained. "One shouldn't think of death."

"I do not think I am really afraid of dying," Devina said reflectively.

As she spoke she realised that someone else had joined them.

"Good-morning, Miss Vanderholtz."

Looking up at him, Devina had to admit that Mr. Thorpe looked his best.

Instead of being huddled into an overcoat like Jake and every other man she had glimpsed so far, with a cap pulled low over his forehead and with rather a "green look about the gills," Mr. Thorpe was different.

He was wearing what she recognised as the boating-jacket with polished crested buttons that was affected by every officer in the Brigade of Guards, and she also noticed that he was wearing the Brigade tie.

She saw, moreover, by the arrangement of the buttons on his jacket that he had been in the Coldstream Guards, while her father had been in the Grenadiers.

'Anyway,' she thought almost regretfully, 'it is something we cannot discuss.'

Galvin Thorpe was bare-headed, and the sunburnt skin on his forehead was in contrast to his dark hair, which waved back from it.

Devina also realised for the first time that he had grey eyes that were the colour of the tempestuous sea.

He was looking at her now with a faint glint of amusement in his eyes as he asked:

"Did I hear you talking about death? Not a suitable subject for anyone during a storm at sea!"

"I was saying that I am not afraid of dying," Devina answered.

"Of course not," he agreed. "It will undoubtedly prove to be another adventure."

He smiled at Nancy-May and without asking per-
mission sat down beside Devina and ignored Jake
Staten.

"Having been in many dangerous situations in my
life," he said now, "I can assure you ladies that if either of you is anxious, there is no danger at this moment, nor is there likely to be any before we reach
Southampton."

"How can you be so sure of that?" Devina asked,
just to be argumentative. "Even big ships like this
could hit an iceberg, or collide with another ship in a
fog."

"I should think the odds against such an occurrence are several million to one," Galvin Thorpe said
dryly. "And think how greatly you would be mourned
if you were drowned before you reached England!"

He spoke with a touch of sarcasm in his voice
which told Devina that once again he was disapproving
of what he thought was her intended marriage to his
cousin.

Because she thought to challenge him she said:

"I was saying to my companion that it is rather
frightening to have someone on board who will be able
to give a report on what I am like before I even reach
your family Castle."

"Do you think that is what I will do?" Galvin
Thorpe enquired.

"I am quite certain of it," Devina answered, "and
I can sense you are critical already."

He turned to look at her and she realised that he
was surprised that she should be so perceptive.

"Why should I be critical?" he asked.

"Why not?" Devina enquired.

Their eyes met and she thought now his expression revealed not only something cynical and perhaps
contemptuous, but a new interest.

It struck her that undoubtedly Galvin Thorpe was
thinking, as many English people did, that all American girls were brash and uncivilised and had little to
recommend them except an inexhaustible fund of dollars.

"I am just hoping, Mr. Thorpe," Devina went on

in a sweet tone, "that if you are making a confidential report it will be an unbiased one."

"I think what you are really trying to say is that it should be impersonal," Galvin Thorpe retorted.

Now there was a definite note of laughter in his voice.

"Perhaps that is too much to expect," Devina said quickly, "but you might try to be just."

He laughed.

"Now you are really coming into the open, Miss Vanderholtz. To accuse me of injustice is surely quite unjustified?"

Devina liked the play on the word but aloud she said:

"I have always been brought up to believe that the one great virtue of the English is their sense of justice."

"The *one?*" he questioned quickly.

"I will be generous and say that I believe there may be several others," Devina replied airily.

Galvin Thorpe rose to his feet.

"I now intend to continue taking my exercise," he said, "but I would like to thank you, Miss Vanderholtz, for giving me a few moments of delightful entertainment."

He bowed, said: "Good-bye, Miss Castleton," and ignored Jake as he had done when he arrived.

Then he walked briskly away down the deck, balancing himself athletically against the roll of the ship.

"Curse him!" Jake said as soon as he was out of hearing. "I'm quite certain he's watching us."

"Why should he do that?" Nancy-May asked. "And, Devina, you were splendid! You stood up to him!"

"These stuck-up limeys are all the same," Jake said disgustedly. "They say one thing and think another. 'Watch their eyes,' my father used to say to me—'a man's eyes can give him away.'"

"What did he mean by that?" Nancy-May asked, curious.

"He meant," Jake said almost savagely, "that a man will smile at you with his lips while his eyes are damning you to hell!"

"Jake!" Nancy-May ejaculated, shocked by his language.

Devina said nothing but she thought that Jake was not of the class he pretended to be.

No gentleman, and certainly not somebody like Galvin Thorpe, who had been in the Brigade of Guards, would have spoken in such a manner in front of two young ladies.

Then she told herself she was being unfair; different countries had different rules of behaviour and she should not judge Jake by British standards.

Jake rose to his feet.

"Come on," he said. "Let's go back to the cabin. That fellow gives me the creeps, and that's the truth!"

"I think everyone we meet is likely to do that," Devina said in a low voice. "It is not their fault, but ours."

She did not wait to hear Jake's reply but moved carefully along the deck until she found a door.

* * *

The following day, when the storm had abated, it was obvious that they would have to go down to meals and to meet Lady Taylor.

She had sent them several polite notes and was also very apologetic because she was being so useless.

Now they learnt that she intended to appear at dinner and hoped they would do the same.

"We have to do so," Devina said firmly. "We cannot eat in our cabin when our Chaperon, who is an older woman, can reach the Dining-Saloon."

"It's so disappointing that Jake can't sit with us," Nancy-May said.

Jake echoed what she said by replying:

"I'm fed up with having to walk two or three paces behind you. It'll be different once we are married and needn't go on pretending all the time."

"No, we'll be together," Nancy-May said, her eyes shining, "and I shall be very proud to be your wife."

"You darling girl! You're a real honey!" Jake replied and kissed her hand.

There was no doubt that in Nancy-May's eyes everything Jake did was perfect, but again Devina was thinking that Nancy-May had no-one with whom to compare him, since she had always been kept away from any young men who might have found her attractive.

Even the guests they entertained at 550 Fifth Avenue had nearly all been elderly, and friends of Mr. and Mrs. Vanderholtz.

There were a few young married couples, it was true, but the married men were certainly not likely to show any interest in Nancy-May.

She had therefore inevitably been swept off her feet by the first man who came along.

'What can I do about it?' Devina wondered for the thousandth time, but could find no answer.

Now they were in smoother waters and it was obvious that everyone was anxious to see everybody else and to look their best.

It was very exciting for Devina to put on one of Nancy-May's exquisite dresses which had cost more than she could have earned in a year or more.

White and silver rouched and draped with tulle and embroidered with diamanté, it was the loveliest gown she had ever imagined.

"You had better wear my diamond necklace," Nancy-May said. "They'll expect you to look rich."

Devina also thought it a good idea although she was terrified of losing anything so valuable.

Nancy-May, in her part as a companion, wore no jewellery with the gown of blue which matched her eyes.

When they met Lady Taylor as arranged in the Saloon it was to find her elaborately gowned and wearing some very fine pearls.

She was a tall, stately woman who looked, Devina thought, exactly as an Ambassadress should, and her greeting was very cordial.

"I am so mortified, dear Miss Vanderholtz," she said, "that I had to stay in my cabin when I should have been introducing you to some charming people and helping you to enjoy yourself."

"I am so sorry you were ill," Devina replied.

Lady Taylor smiled.

"*Mal de mer,* as the French call it most appropriately, is very undignified, and therefore very lowering, but now the worst is over and I am trying to forget it ever happened."

She was charming to Nancy-May, which made Devina know she had a kind heart, and then they all swept down to the Captain's table.

Lady Taylor sat on his right, and on her other side there was a Hungarian diplomat whom she knew well.

Devina had the Hungarian on her left, and there was an empty seat on her right, which was filled by Galvin Thorpe a few minutes after she had sat down.

She had almost anticipated that this might happen, because she felt sure that Lady Taylor would have intimated to whoever organised the seating arrangements that it would be nice for them to get to know each other.

There was no doubt in Devina's mind that Mrs. Vanderholtz would have confided in Lady Taylor, of course under a vow of secrecy, who Nancy-May was to marry.

Nancy-May, in her role as the unimportant Miss Castleton, was between two young men, one an Irishman who had been in America on business, the other a French diplomat who was being chaffed by other people at the table for not travelling on his own country's famous ship *la Savole*.

He obviously found Nancy-May attractive and paid her fulsome compliments from the moment dinner started.

It brought a flush to her cheeks and a light to her eyes, and Devina was certain that she was finding her freedom, without the strict chaperonage of her mother, something delightfully new.

It was, however, difficult to concentrate on Nancy-May when Mr. Thorpe was beside her.

"What have you been doing today?" he asked. "Or is that a banal question?"

"I have been reading," Devina answered truthfully.

"Surely there are many other entertainments on board in which you could have joined?"

"I have always thought that it is wiser to look upon a sea voyage as a sort of rest-cure," Devina said evasively.

"That may apply to most people, but not you!"

"Why not?" Devina asked in surprise.

"Because the whole ship is agog to meet the wealthy Miss Vanderholtz," he said.

Devina was sure that once again he was speaking with a touch of sarcasm in his voice, and she replied:

"I would like to believe that, Mr. Thorpe, but I am in fact immune to compliments which are too exaggerated to be credible."

Galvin Thorpe laughed and it was spontaneously natural.

"I think, Miss Vanderholtz," he said, "that you are trying to snub me, and quite frankly I find that a new experience."

Devina was sure this was true.

He was, she thought, far too attractive for him not to have had many women running after him and striving to amuse him and to capture him. But certainly they had not snubbed him.

"I . . . I was not really snubbing you," she said, remembering that they had decided to be nice to him. "It was just, I suppose, as my father would have said, that the English cannot take compliments."

Even as she spoke she realised she had made a ghastly error and wondered frantically how she could extricate herself.

He had not missed her point.

"The English?" he asked in a puzzled voice.

"As you are English, I was trying not to be complimentary," Devina explained rather lamely.

"I can assure you that in my very strenuous journeys of exploration," Galvin Thorpe said, "I get very few compliments and a great deal of kicks."

Devina gave a sigh of relief.

She had fallen into a pit of her own making, but somehow she had extricated herself.

'I must be more careful . . . much more careful!'

she thought, and decided it would be a mistake to have another duel of wits with Galvin Thorpe.

There was, however, something very exhilarating in challenging him and defying that look of criticism in his eyes and the dry, sarcastic note in his voice.

With a sense of relief she turned to the diplomat on her other side, and by flattering him with her obvious attention and expressing an almost fulsome interest in everything he said to her she managed to keep him talking to her until nearly the end of the meal.

Then, because the diplomat was forced to speak to Lady Taylor, she had to turn once again to Galvin Thorpe.

He looked at her speculatively for a moment, then he said:

"Well, have you decided?"

"Decided what?"

"Whether you will continue to look on me as an enemy or accept me as a friend."

"I think that is up to . . . you," she said in a low voice. "I thought when you first came to call on me that you were . . . definitely hostile."

"You are very perceptive, Miss Vanderholtz—for an American!"

"And you are particularly frightening as an Englishman," Devina replied.

He laughed and said:

"I think tonight at any rate the victory is yours! Shall we call a truce?"

"As long as it is not a trick to make me lay down my arms while you retain yours," Devina said.

"I promise to throw away my weapons," he replied. "And I would like to be your friend."

There was a note in his voice which made her look at him in surprise.

Then as his grey eyes met hers she knew he was speaking the truth and was no longer hostile.

The battle, if there had been one, was over.

She felt a sudden warmth that had not been there before. Then, as she would have spoken again, Lady Taylor rose to lead them from the Dining-Saloon.

Chapter Four

Devina was alone in the cabin, Nancy-May and Jake having gone out on deck. Things had been very difficult and she gave a little sigh of relief.

Nancy-May was having a success with the people she met at the Captain's table and through them a number of other gentlemen.

Devina was aware that while people, out of sheer curiosity, wished to meet her because they thought she was Miss Vanderholtz, the younger set gravitated naturally towards the vivacious gaiety of Nancy-May.

It resulted, of course, in Jake becoming extremely jealous.

He made scenes, and only when Nancy-May flung herself into his arms to assure him over and over again how much she loved him did he quiet down and make love to her in the way she enjoyed.

Devina found it all very nerve-racking, especially as she was afraid that Jake's jealousy might result in him and Nancy-May doing something so stupid in public that the whole deception would be exposed.

Lady Taylor had been so kind and had taken so much trouble over her that it pricked her conscience considerably to know that the Ambassadress was being deceived.

And although she had made friends with Galvin Thorpe she was still afraid of the penetrating look in his eyes and the manner in which she felt he was watching her.

This was, she knew, due to the fact that he was sizing her up as a wife for his cousin, but she was well aware that he was too shrewd not to notice any little slip that might give her away.

She had quite commendably remembered occasionally to say a word or a sentence in the typically American manner in which she would be expected to speak.

She glossed over any mistakes Nancy-May might make by telling everyone that Miss Castleton had lived in America for so long that she had in fact become "Americanised."

"I am sure everything is going well," Devina told herself.

While in one way she knew it would be a relief to arrive at Southampton, she was well aware that many more problems and difficulties awaited her there.

She had managed to convince Galvin Thorpe who she was, but it was going to be much more difficult, she felt, to convince the Dowager Duchess and the Duke.

She also wondered what Galvin Thorpe would have to tell them about her.

As if the thought of him conjured him up, there was a knock on the door and before she could answer he came into the cabin.

"I imagined you would be alone," he said, "for I saw Miss Castleton on deck, surrounded by an admiring throng."

"Surrounded by . . . what?" Devina asked.

"Young men, of course. I gather she has rather a penchant for them."

"I am so glad she is being a success," Devina said.

Galvin Thorpe laughed.

"You sound like an elderly Dowager chaperoning a débutante. Do you not wish to have a good time yourself?"

"I am having a wonderful time!" Devina answered in all sincerity.

Galvin Thorpe would not understand that to travel in such luxury, to meet people like Lady Taylor and the diplomats whom she sat next to at mealtimes, was, after a long year of nursing her aunt, like walking out into the sunshine.

In Samuel Keeward's gloomy house there had been no intelligent conversation, no discussions of world affairs, and certainly no friendliness.

She wondered what Galvin Thorpe would say if she told him that a little over a week ago she had been wondering where her next meal would come from and how long it would be before her hands, made raw by so much washing and scrubbing, would grow soft again.

Instead she said:

"I see you have brought me your sketches."

"You assured me that you really wanted to see them."

"And so I do. Your stories of your experiences in the Sudan have fascinated me, but it is difficult to visualise what one does not actually see with one's own eyes."

He smiled as he handed her a sketch-book, then watched her as she turned over the pages.

Because she knew it was important not to talk about herself or to let Galvin Thorpe probe too far into her past, she had encouraged him to talk about his explorations.

She had discovered that he had been in the Province of Bahr al-Ghazal in the Sudan.

He told her about the customs and beliefs of the natives, and when she discovered that he had drawn sketches of the Dinkas, who he said were one of the most beautiful tribes in the world, she had asked to see them.

Now as she looked at the drawings of slim, elegant natives who legend averred had Grecian blood in them, she could understand his interest in them.

When Galvin Thorpe talked of the life he had lived among them there was an enthusiastic warmth in his voice which was not there at other times.

"But you are an artist!" she exclaimed.

"I only wish that were true!" he said. "There is so much that I have not the capability to portray on paper, but perhaps words will be able to express it better in my book."

"The women are beautiful!"

"That is what I thought, but to persuade them to model for me I had to buy them."

"Buy them?" Devina exclaimed, confused.

"Their parents refused to see the difference between a 'model' and a wife," Galvin Thorpe explained. "It is not that they took up a moral attitude; they simply mistrusted this new-fangled word 'model' and suspected that they would be cheated out of their right."

"So these girls became your wives?" Devina questioned.

"Aneegi," he said, pointing with his finger at the sketch, "was twelve or fourteen, no-one was quite certain, and she cost six cows, or approximately four pounds. Rafa cost less."

Devina could not help smiling.

"She was certainly a very cheap wife."

"It was the going rate in Tonj."

"Your wife would certainly cost you more in New York or London."

"At what value would you put yourself?" he asked.

Now there was that cynical sarcasm in his voice which Devina had heard before.

She knew that the answer was "a coronet"!

She put down the sketch-book and walked across the room to where there were some drinks on a side-table.

Jake has insisted on this, so that the stewards would not be suspicious that he was always drinking with the heiress whom he was supposed to be guarding.

There was a pause.

"You have not answered my question," Galvin Thorpe prompted.

"I see no necessity for doing so," Devina replied coldly.

"Actually I would like an answer. Why are you doing this? Can you possibly expect to be happy in such circumstances?"

Devina did not answer and he went on:

"I imagined when I learnt you were on board that I would find a frivolous, empty-headed girl who had no interests outside the Social World, but you are different."

"I see no . . . point in this . . . discussion," Devina said in a low voice.

"There is a point," he said violently, "and I wish to discuss it! You have, and I admit it, brains and intelligence and a sensitivity I have known in few women."

He paused before he went on:

"How then can you contemplate a life based on the primitive purchase of a wife as practised by savages?"

His voice seemed to ring out round the cabin. Then there was a silence which seemed to vibrate between them.

"There is . . . nothing I can . . . say," Devina murmured in a low voice.

"I am well aware, knowing my aunt, that she has arranged this monstrous deal with your mother," Galvin Thorpe said. "I have always suspected that she had had such a thing in mind ever since my cousin grew up. But, as I have already said, you are different."

Devina had not been able to look at him as he spoke but instead stood at the table staring blindly at the glasses, the bottles of gin and whisky, and the shining top of the soda-syphon.

Galvin Thorpe walked across the cabin towards her.

"Listen to me," he said. "Pull out of this engagement before it is announced. Go back to America, or on to Paris, but do not allow yourself to be pressured into a marriage which when you are older you may regret bitterly."

Devina made no response. She could not move, she could only go on staring blindly in front of her.

"I know that every American mother's ambition is to have a Duke in the family," he said, "just as your over-vaunted dollars appeal to the English. The combination may work in some instances, but not with you."

He paused before he went on:

"You are buying for yourself a glittering bauble, but with it goes unhappiness and loneliness of spirit."

His voice had deepened and Devina felt as if it vibrated through her. Then with an effort to stop him from saying any more she pleaded:

"Please . . . I cannot . . . listen to you . . . and I cannot help . . . feeling that you are also being extremely . . . disloyal to your . . . cousin."

"If you think Robert has any part in this, then you are mistaken," Galvin said. "I doubt if he is even yet aware of your arrival."

Devina raised her face and looked at him in a startled manner.

"What are you . . . saying to . . . me?"

"I am telling you that this arrangement—or whatever you like to call it—has been planned by my aunt. My cousin is a pleasant, trusting young man who will find himself walking down the aisle with you before he has time to catch his breath."

"And would that be such a terrible thing?" Devina asked angrily.

"Not for him, but for you," Galvin Thorpe replied.

"So you are really thinking of . . . me?"

"I thought I had made that clear."

Devina drew in her breath.

"I suppose I ought to thank you, but actually you are . . . interfering in things which do not concern you, so I will ask you . . . not to speak of . . . this again."

"Which means that you intend to purchase a Ducal coronet and that you believe it will give you everything you want in life."

There was a pause before Galvin went on angrily:

"Well, let me tell you, if you do you will regret it bitterly!"

"That is for me to decide," Devina said, and hoped she sounded cold and dignified.

As it happened, the way that Galvin Thorpe was ranting made her feel strangely weak and at the same

time receptive to him in a manner she did not understand.

She could not think clearly nor could she understand why he was so concerned.

She only knew that the violence and rawness of
his voice seemed to ignite a response within her that
was something she had never felt before.

"I suppose I am being a fool in thinking that anything I can say would make any difference," Galvin
Thorpe was saying in a bitter tone.

Devina did not reply.

Then suddenly and without saying any more he
walked out of the cabin and slammed the door.

For a moment she could not move. Then she sat
down in a chair and put her hands up to her face.

He had disturbed her in a manner that she had
never experienced previously, and for some unaccount-
able reason she felt suddenly near to tears.

Then she told herself that he had said exactly the
things any decent man would say.

Had she really been Miss Vanderholtz, she would
have been wise to listen to him and to refuse to sell
herself in the way that Mrs. Vanderholtz had planned
for Nancy-May.

'Perhaps Nancy-May is right to marry Jake, who
loves her only for herself,' Devina thought.

Then some instinct within herself argued that
that was not really the solution.

Nancy-May was so young and in many ways so
immature.

What did she know of life, men, or indeed of
marriage? She thought herself in love, but was she
really?

And underneath that veneer of charm and persua-
sion what was Jake Staten really like?

She felt as if Galvin Thorpe had forced her to
think more deeply, not of herself but of Nancy-
May.

Perhaps he would approve her courageousness in
running away from a loveless marriage founded on
the exchange of assets and nothing else.

But was it really the answer to marry a man of

whom in many respects she knew less than she did about the Duke?

Who were Jake's parents? What sort of home had he come from? Had he money of his own, as he had told Nancy-May? Or was he just gambling on having a very rich wife to keep him?

Devina wondered what would happen if she went to Galvin Thorpe, told him the truth, and asked him to solve the problem that confronted her.

Then she knew that if she did so she would feel she had betrayed a trust.

'We must go on as we are,' she thought. 'I can only pray that Nancy-May will find happiness in the life she has chosen.'

She was still sitting there, thinking, and feeling as if everything was going round and round in her mind, when Nancy-May came into the cabin.

"I played a game of quoit and I won!" she said. "Such a nice man partnered me, and I promised to dance with him this evening."

"Who is he?" Devina asked automatically.

"I haven't the slightest idea," Nancy-May answered. "Everyone calls him Billy, so I called him Billy too."

Devina could not help thinking how horrified Mrs. Vanderholtz would be if she knew of the casual way in which Nancy-May was behaving.

However, she thought it was perhaps a good thing that Nancy-May should not confine herself entirely to being with Jake.

At that moment Jake came into the cabin.

"Why did you rush off?" he asked. "I was there waiting for you and I only went into the Bar for a quick drink."

"I couldn't see you anywhere," Nancy-May replied, "so I came here."

"That was sensible," Devina approved. "I am sure your mother would not like you to roam about the ship unaccompanied."

"Are you telling me that I'm not doing my duty?" Jake asked with a rather nasty note in his voice.

"I am merely saying that Mrs. Vanderholtz told

me that Nancy-May was never to be alone," Devina replied. "The next time I had better come with her."

"I can look after her without any assistance," Jake retorted.

"Of course you can!" Nancy-May cried. "You know I only want to be with you, but I couldn't very well refuse to play quoit when the Deck-Master asked me to."

"No, of course not," Devina said soothingly before Jake could speak. "Why not come and change before luncheon? There is something I want to tell you."

"What's that?" Jake asked sharply.

"Secrets!" Devina replied tantalisingly. "All women have them, you will find."

Jake looked surly as he walked towards the drinks, and Devina linking her arm through Nancy-May's went with her into her State-Room.

"What do you want to tell me?" Nancy-May asked.

"I only wanted to warn you," Devina said, "that Mr. Thorpe came here when you were on deck and begged me to give up the idea of marrying his cousin."

"Why should he do that?" Nancy-May asked.

"He seems to think there is no chance of the marriage being successful, since I, or rather you, and the Duke know so little about each other."

"Well, as I'm not going to marry the Duke, it doesn't matter what Mr. Thorpe thinks," Nancy-May retorted.

"I know," Devina answered. "At the same time, I thought you ought to know what he felt."

"I couldn't care less what he feels!"

Nancy-May sat down on the bed.

"I'm having a wonderful time, Devina, and it's really rather exciting making Jake so jealous. He absolutely glowers when other men pay attention to me."

"You are quite certain you love him enough to marry him?" Devina enquired.

"Quite, quite certain! All these men on the ship are fun, and I like their making a fuss of me, but it's Jake I love! It's Jake I want to marry!"

"Then I hope you will be very, very happy!"

"Why do you say it like that?" Nancy-May asked.

"It is just what Mr. Thorpe said about people getting married because they each have something to gain from it."

Nancy-May was silent for a moment, then she said:

"You're thinking again that Jake has so much to gain from me!"

"He has!" Devina answered. "And that is why I would like you to wait a little. You see what a success you are when nobody knows that you are Miss Vanderholtz! Meet the Duke, and then if you do not like him, refuse to marry him!"

She saw that Nancy-May was listening, and she pleaded:

"Let us go to Paris or Venice and see a little of the world before you return to America."

"It sounds rather fun," Nancy-May replied, "but not as exciting as being married to Jake! And now that we've made all the plans about going to Scotland, how could we possibly change them?"

"Quite easily!" Devina said eagerly.

"And what will Mr. Thorpe say when he knows I am you and you are me?"

"Oh, we will explain that you wanted to have fun and thought you would be less restricted if you changed places with me."

Nancy-May laughed and got off the bed to kiss Devina.

"You're sweet," she said, "and I love you! But Jake warned me you'd try and twist me out of marrying him, and he was right!"

"Why should he think I would do that?" Devina asked.

"He said you were a conventional, stuffy Britisher at heart, and they always disapprove of anything adventurous."

"A run-away marriage is rather more than that," Devina said.

"I agree with you, and that's why I intend to run away with Jake!" Nancy-May cried triumphantly.

Devina felt depressingly that there was nothing more she could do.

She knew that Nancy-May had related to Jake what had taken place between them, because later in the day he was brusque to the point of rudeness, and she guessed he now regarded her as an enemy.

At the same time, she told herself consolingly that he could not afford to quarrel with her until he and Nancy-May were on their way to Scotland.

The next day was their last on board and there were all sorts of games and competitions taking place amongst the younger passengers and a Gala Dinner was arranged for the evening.

Nancy-May was very excited at the idea, but for some reason which she could not herself understand Devina felt too worried and depressed to be excited about anything.

It was stupid, she knew, and she kept telling herself that she would never see this sort of life again.

When she was struggling to find employment or living with one of her elderly cousins, she would regret the time she had wasted worrying about Nancy-May.

Then she realised frankly there was more to it than that.

It was only later in the afternoon, when she was walking on deck with Nancy-May beside her and Jake trailing a little way behind, that she understood what was wrong.

Galvin Thorpe was leaning over the rail, looking out to sea, and as Devina saw him she felt her heart turn a somersault in her breast.

'How can I be so absurd?' she wondered, and knew the answer.

Galvin Thorpe greeted them with a smile.

"The last day of the voyage," he said. "Are you looking forward to seeing England for the first time?"

For a moment Devina was so bemused at what she had suddenly learnt about herself that she could only look at him vaguely, and then with an effort she managed to answer:

"Y-yes . . . yes, of course!"

A ship's officer came over and started to talk to Nancy-May, and Galvin Thorpe said in a low voice:

"Have you forgiven me for what I said to you yesterday?"

"I realised you were ... thinking of ... me and trying to be ... kind," Devina replied.

"I thought afterwards that I had gone the wrong way about it," he said. "Women always want to be coaxed, not driven."

He looked down into her eyes and added so that only she could hear:

"Is that what you want?"

She felt as if every nerve in her body responded to him in a way that was almost frightening.

Because she was shy, because she was bewildered by the intensity of her feeling, she could only reply:

"N-no ... of course ... not."

"Will you dance with me tonight?"

"I do not ... know. Perhaps it will be ... impossible."

"Why should it be that? I assure you I am a good dancer."

"It is ... difficult to make any ... plans."

She felt that she was being helplessly stupid. Then, to her relief, Nancy-May finished her conversation with the ship's officer and interposed:

"Hello, Mr. Thorpe. Why didn't you come down to dinner last night?"

It was a question Devina herself had been longing to ask him.

"I was invited to dine in a private party," Galvin Thorpe answered, "and the guests included several men whom I found very interesting."

"What about the ladies?" Nancy-May enquired.

"It was a bachelor-party," Galvin Thorpe replied.

"That sounds very dull," she said as she giggled.

A week ago, Devina thought, Nancy-May would never have behaved so easily or so naturally with a man as she was able to do now.

The ship's journey had, if nothing else, opened

new horizons for the American girl, just as it had for
Devina herself.

She had thought last night when Galvin Thorpe
did not come down to dinner that the reason was that
he was angry with her. Yet, after all he had said, he
had doubtless put her out of his mind.

It was what she told herself she wanted him to do,
but her heart told her something different.

"Oh, come on!" Nancy-May said. "Let's go and
watch the badminton."

As they moved away Devina told herself that when
Galvin Thorpe ultimately found out how fundamen-
tally she had deceived him, he would certainly never
wish to speak to her again.

When evening came, balloons, paper streamers,
and party-hats were distributed in the Dining-Hall and
it looked very festive before they went up to the Saloon
to dance.

Devina sat down beside Lady Taylor.

"Your companion, Miss Castleton, is certainly a
great success," the Ambassadress said in her charming
voice.

Devina had noticed how many men had clustered
round Nancy-May, asking for dances, and she had in
fact wondered why so few approached herself.

As if Lady Taylor read her thoughts, she said:

"I think you will understand, Miss Vanderholtz,
that most gentlemen are nervous of asking you to
dance."

"Why should they be?"

Lady Taylor smiled.

"They are afraid of being accused of being for-
tune-hunters. That is one of the penalties of being
very rich. The right sort of men never wish to appear
pushing."

"The right sort of men!" Devina repeated under
her breath. That certainly did not apply to Jake.

She glanced round to see where he was, quite
certain that he would be in some corner of the room
staring jealously at Nancy-May.

Then to her astonishment she saw him dancing
with her.

'That is a mistake,' she thought, then told herself that perhaps no-one would realise who he was.

She was sure, however, that it would not have escaped the searching eyes of Galvin Thorpe.

He came up to Lady Taylor, greeted her, talked politely for a few seconds, and then said:

"May I ask Miss Vanderholtz for a dance?"

"Of course," Lady Taylor agreed.

Devina rose a little nervously.

"I am afraid," she said as Galvin Thorpe put his arm round her, "that I have not danced for some time and I may find it difficult to follow you."

"I thought Americans did little else but dance," he teased.

Devina did not answer. She was in fact concentrating on the dancing, which seemed to have changed since she had been to young people's parties in England.

But, as Galvin Thorpe had said himself, he was a good dancer. She found that they moved smoothly together and she was not stumbling over his feet as she had feared.

"I knew you would dance well," he said.

"How could you have known that?"

"It is the way you move—and also you have instinct, as I have."

"That makes me feel . . . nervous."

"Why? Are you afraid I will find out things which you wish to keep secret?"

Devina drew in her breath.

That was the truth, she knew, although he was speaking lightly.

"I am always afraid of people who are so intuitive that they can read one's thoughts," she said, "or are so clairvoyant that they are able to read the future."

"Then I will do neither," he said. "But I will tell you that you waltz divinely, or else we are particularly attuned to each other."

That was the real truth, Devina thought. She was attuned to him, whatever he might think about her.

It gave her a feeling of intense excitement to be

close to him, to feel his arm round her, his hand holding hers.

There was something very intimate about dancing together.

Because she felt strange sensations she had never known before pulsating in her breast, she was almost glad when the dance came to an end and he took her back to Lady Taylor.

"You dance so well together!" the British Ambassadress exclaimed. "When I was young my husband and I used to be thought of as the best dancers in the Ball-Room. I remember we grew rather conceited about it!"

"Will you dance with me now?" Galvin Thorpe asked.

Lady Taylor shook her head.

"I have given up dancing," she said. "But it still delights me to see young people enjoying it so much."

As she spoke, a very old man who looked like a tortoise was propelling a fat woman, his partner, passed them, and they laughed.

"It is always wise in life to know when to stop," Lady Taylor said with a smile.

"That is something I was telling Miss Vanderholtz only yesterday!" Galvin Thorpe said.

Devina looked at him indignantly and the colour rose in her cheeks as she wondered how he dared refer to the angry way in which he had ranted at her.

Someone stopped to speak to him at that moment and Devina made her mind up to go to bed.

She wanted so much to stay, wanted so desperately to dance with him, but she knew she must run away, not from him but from herself.

She made her excuses to Lady Taylor and went down to her cabin.

Only when she was alone in her luxurious State-Room did she put her hands up to her face and ask herself how she could be so foolish, so ridiculous, as to fall in love.

What was the point of loving a man who despised her already and would undoubtedly despise her even

more when he knew how she had deceived him and
everyone else?

What was more, he would feel she had made a
fool of him, and no man would ever forgive that.

He had said they might be friends, but she was
sure that that was only a manner of speaking.

Despite the occasional pleasant things he said, she
knew by the expression in his eyes what he really
thought.

"How, in the circumstances, can I be such a fool
as to love him?" she asked herself.

But she knew that the strange feelings which possessed her the moment he appeared, the sensations
which rippled through her when he touched her, and
the wonder of dancing with him, meant only one thing
—love.

It was something she had never felt before in
her whole life.

"I am . . . mistaken. It is just because I like . . .
sparring with him. I like the stimulation of fighting
with him verbally," she told herself.

But she knew she was not mistaken; and, as if
there were not enough problems and difficulties ahead,
this, because it was hers and hers alone, seemed for
the moment worse than all the others.

She had told herself earlier in the day that when
they reached Southampton she would never see Galvin Thorpe again, but when he had sat down to dinner
he had said:

"You may be interested to hear that I have wire-
lessed my cousin from the ship and have tonight received a reply."

Devina waited tensely for what he was going to
say.

"He has of course asked me to escort you to the
Castle," Galvin Thorpe went on, "and has invited me
to stay there as long as I wish."

Devina drew in her breath.

Here was an added complication.

There had, however, been so much noise in the
Dining-Saloon from those celebrating the last night of

the voyage that she had not had time until now to think about what Galvin Thorpe's information entailed.

She put her hands up to her forehead in an effort to think clearly.

Jake's plan had been that he and Nancy-May would leave her and Rose at Southampton and start immediately on their journey to Scotland.

She would go to Milnthorpe Castle without them.

Mrs. Vanderholtz had expected that there would be a Courier sent by the Duke to meet them.

"His Grace will not come himself," she had said confidently, "but will wait to greet you on your arrival at the Castle."

"Do we go by train?" Nancy-May had asked.

"There will be a special railway-carriage reserved for you," Mrs. Vanderholtz answered, "and carriages waiting at the station nearest to the Castle."

It all sounded very easy, and Devina's only question then had been when she was expected to leave Nancy-May once they arrived in England.

She had asked Mrs. Vanderholtz about this.

"It rather depends on Nancy-May. She may require you to instruct her in the etiquette at the Castle. Just wait and see what she needs, and of course you will be paid for any extra time you are with her."

Devina had been quite content with that, but now she was forced to consider what she would say to Galvin Thorpe if Nancy-May and Jake disappeared at Southampton.

One complication would undoubtedly be that Miss Vanderholtz would not be expected to travel unchaperoned with a man.

"We shall have to discuss this and think about it very seriously," Devina told herself.

She did not undress but sat waiting in the Sitting-Room for several hours.

She was not asleep when finally Nancy-May and Jake came into the cabin, wearing paper hats on their heads, and Jake was carrying a whole armful of carnival favours, balloons, and other objects they had collected during the evening.

"Are you still up?" Nancy-May exclaimed when she saw Devina. "I can't think why you left so early."

"I was worried," Devina said. "And there is something I have to tell you both."

"What's that?" Jake asked.

He threw everything he carried down in an armchair and crossed the room towards the drinks table.

"Oh, stop drinking for a moment and listen to what Devina has to say," Nancy-May said.

"Is anything wrong?" Jake asked, and his voice was sharp.

Devina replied bluntly:

"Mr. Thorpe has been invited to the Castle and asked to escort us there from Southampton!"

"Hell and damnation!" Jake swore. "Isn't that just like him, butting in where he's not wanted!"

"Does that mean we can't start off for Scotland as we intended?" Nancy-May asked.

"I don't see why we should change our plans to suit him!" Jake replied aggressively.

"The difficulty is that he, and particularly the Dowager Duchess, will think it very strange for me to travel unchaperoned, without a companion," Devina explained.

"Then you must get yourself one," Jake said, "because Nancy-May is coming with me."

"I do not see how I can . . ." Devina began, only to be interrupted as he said angrily:

"This is what you've been scheming for all along —isn't it? To stop Nancy-May from marrying me! And you're using this as an excuse."

"That is not true!" Devina protested. "How was I to know Mr. Thorpe would be asked to stay at the Castle?"

"Perhaps you prompted him into inviting himself."

"I did nothing of the sort!" Devina replied more calmly. "And I can assure you that it was a great surprise when he told me at dinner that he had wirelessed the Duke, who had replied with the invitation."

Jake swore again, but under his breath.

Nancy-May put out her hands towards Devina, asking:

"What can we do? We must go to Scotland!"

There was a silence until Jake said:

"Wait a minute. Let me think. I've got to have all the brains on this trip, I can see that!"

Then he said slowly to Devina:

"You say you ought to have a companion with you—what's wrong with Rose?"

"Rose is a servant. She would not travel in the same compartment as Mr. Thorpe and myself."

"Oh, I see! The class differences of England! I might have guessed we'd come up against them sooner or later."

Devina did not deign to reply and after a moment he said:

"What the hell does it matter what they think about you? When they find out you're not Miss Vanderholtz but only a penniless hanger-on, they'll kick you down the Castle steps anyway!"

The way he spoke made Devina decide there was no point in trying to argue with him.

"Very well," she said. "I will go alone with Mr. Thorpe. But you will have to think of a good reason why Nancy-May cannot accompany me."

Jake clapped his hands together.

"That's it! That's it exactly!" he said. "Nancy-May can't go with you because . . ."

He put his hand up to his chin and repeated:

"Because—because she's received a telegram at Southampton to say her aged British mother is ill and wants to see her immediately. How's that?"

"I suppose it is as good an explanation as any other," Devina said coldly.

Nancy-May jumped up from the sofa on which she had been sitting to fling her arms round his neck.

"You're so clever, Jake! I knew you'd think of something! I was frightened . . . terrified for a moment that we wouldn't be able to get away!"

"I told you to leave everything to me," Jake replied. "We're going to be married, honey, and nothing and no-one's going to stop us—least of all some toffee-nosed British ideas which no intelligent people would tolerate for an instant!"

Devina had no intention of rising to the bait. Instead she said:

"Well, I am glad that is settled, but naturally I was worried. That is why I waited up to see you."

"That was sweet of you," Nancy-May said quickly. "Wasn't it, Jake?"

"I'm sure you meant it for the best," he said coolly.

"Good-night, Nancy-May," Devina said, and opened the door of her State-Room. But Nancy-May ran after her and kissed her.

"Thank you, Devina," she said. "You've been a sport about everything, and Jake and I are very grateful, we are really."

Devina went into her State-Room and shut the door.

She knew now that she disliked Jake and also mistrusted him, but what could she do about it?

Supposing now at the last moment she tried to get in touch with Mrs. Vanderholtz?

But even if she did, it would be too late.

They would dock at Southampton early tomorrow morning, and then Jake would whisk Nancy-May off to Scotland.

They had already planned that as soon as they were married they would wire Devina at the Castle, and then she would be able to extract herself from her uncomfortable position as quickly as possible.

Now Devina told herself it was far worse than she had anticipated.

It would be bad enough to explain what had happened to the Duke and his doubtless frustrated and angry mother. But the thought of facing the contempt and disgust of Galvin Thorpe was more than she could bear.

She had seen that look of contempt so clearly in his eyes when they had first met, and she had heard the anger and disgust in his voice when he had denounced her for selling herself for a coronet.

"What will he say and what will he think when he

knows I am a cheat and a liar?" she asked herself. "I cannot bear it!"

She wondered wildly whether she too should try to disappear at Southampton.

If Jake could think of plausible explanations for their disappearance, why could she not find one for herself?

Then she knew that if for one moment the Press suspected that Miss Vanderholtz had vanished, the whole of England would be looking for her.

It would be very unlikely in that case that either she, Nancy-May, or Jake would get very far without being recognised.

Devina had been very careful not to be photographed or interviewed by any of the reporters on board ship.

But the reporters, who were always taking notes, had taken snap-shots of Nancy-May on the badminton-court, playing quoit, and socialising with various groups of people.

The British newspapers were still very interested in Britain's newest and greatest passenger ship.

"I shall have to go to the Castle," Devina decided.

She felt it was not only a question of being afraid; there was also something that made her feel ecstatic and excited because she would be with Galvin Thorpe for just a little longer.

"I love him!" she murmured, and then she wondered why love, which to most people was a time of happiness and joy, was to her an agony tinged with fear.

"I love him!" she repeated to herself as she undressed and got into bed.

She tried to make herself think that this was the last time she would ever know such luxury, such comfort, and that she should savour it.

But instead all she could see was Galvin Thorpe's face, and feel the pressure of his arm round her waist and the closeness of her hand in his.

She wondered what it would be like to be still

closer to him, to know that both his arms enfolded her, to feel his lips on hers.

Then, ashamed of her own thoughts, she turned her face against the pillow, only to hear her mind and heart repeating over and over again:

"I love him! I love him!"

Chapter Five

Everything was confusion at Southampton, which made it easier, Devina felt, for Galvin Thorpe not to realise what was happening.

Jake had arranged that he and Nancy-May would step ashore from the Second-Class gangway as soon as the ship had docked.

Devina said that she would stay in her cabin as long as possible so that she would not have to explain what had happened to the run-aways before she had actually left the ship.

Nancy-May had decided that Devina must take the bulk of her luggage with her to Milnthorpe Castle.

After the whole plot had been disclosed she could arrange for the Duke to send the trunks on to London, where Nancy-May would pick them up on their return from Scotland.

This meant, Devina told herself, that, difficult although everything would be, at least she could wear beautiful gowns and enjoy the confidence that they gave her.

Unfortunately, with every moment that drew her nearer to the time when she would arrive in England pretending to be someone else and have to explain to Galvin Thorpe why she must travel with him alone, she felt more and more nervous.

She was unable to sleep and lay tossing in the comfortable bed in her State-Room, going over and over in her mind everything she must say, until finally she felt more and more confused, and more afraid of facing the final denouement.

Nancy-May also found it hard to sleep, and she came into Devina's cabin very early.

"Are you awake, Devina?" she asked from the door in a whisper.

"Yes, of course," Devina answered, sitting up in bed and turning on the light.

Nancy-May sat down beside her.

"I'm excited," she said, "and yet for the first time since I left New York I'm asking myself if I'm doing the right thing."

"If there is any question about it, tell yourself 'no'!" Devina begged. "Please, Nancy-May, give yourself more time."

"And supposing, if I do, Jake doesn't wait for me?" Nancy-May replied.

Devina longed to reply that Jake would not give up her millions so easily, but she was too tactful to say anything except:

"If he loves you, he will wait."

"He loves me and I love him," Nancy-May said, "but I'm not certain if I've seen enough of the world to settle down yet as a married woman with a dozen children."

She spoke in such a comical way that Devina laughed.

"You do not have to have a dozen all at once!"

Nancy-May laughed too, but it was a somewhat subdued sound.

"I really thought over what you suggested to me," she said after a moment, "but you know as well as I do that if I don't marry the Duke as Momma intends, I shall be whisked back to New York."

She sighed before she continued:

"I'd be shut away from everybody as I've been before, and what help is that? Besides, I think it'd kill Momma after all the trouble she's had to find me a Ducal bridegroom."

"People do not die so easily," Devina said a little sarcastically.

"Momma's often told me that Mrs. Vanderbilt

very nearly died of a heart-attack when Consuela wanted to marry some young man she'd met and not the Duke of Marlborough."

"I heard," Devina replied, "that Mrs. Vanderbilt threatened to shoot a man in whom her daughter was interested."

Nancy-May considered this for a moment.

"I can't see Momma trying to shoot Jake, but she might make Poppa do it!"

Devina did not speak, and Nancy-May cried:

"How could I bear that? How could I have his blood on my hands when I love him so much?"

"I think you are just frightening yourself with bogeys, which really do not exist," Devina said. "Come with me in the train, Nancy-May, and we will explain to Mr. Thorpe why we changed places. I feel sure he would be very understanding."

Nancy-May was silent as Devina went on pleadingly:

"Think how interesting it would be to meet the Duke and see the Castle, even if you do not marry him. You have never seen a really grand English house. They are very, very impressive, and also very beautiful."

Nancy-May jumped up from the bed.

"You're tempting me," she said, "but I couldn't break Jake's heart and let him down at this very last moment."

She smiled and it made her look very pretty as she added:

"Think what a romantic story it'll be to tell my grandchildren—a run-away marriage to Gretna Green!"

"Is that where you are going to be married?" Devina asked.

"I think so, but I really don't know. Jake's got all the information and all the papers that he says are necessary."

Nancy-May stretched her hands above her head.

"It doesn't matter where we are married! It's that I shall belong to Jake and never again be prevented

from doing the things I want to do, never again be
watched by detectives and told that I must sell myself
for a title."

"You might find being married to Jake equally
restricting," Devina said quickly. "After all, Jake is
very jealous."

"I like his being jealous," Nancy-May said with
a little smile. "And once we are married I know I
shall never look at another man."

She sat down at the dressing-table and stared at
her face in the mirror, putting her head a little to one
side.

"Do you think I'm pretty, Devina? Really pretty?"

"Of course you are," Devina answered, "and Jake
or no Jake, there will always be men to tell you
so."

"I hope so," Nancy-May said simply. "Do you
know what I heard someone say yesterday?"

"What did you hear?"

"It was a man, and he said: 'Yes, that Castleton
girl's pretty, but the Vanderholtz girl has a spirituality
about her which I find, considering who she is, rather
intriguing.' "

Devina looked at Nancy-May in surprise.

"Did someone really say that?"

"I promise you it's the truth."

"Then I am very flattered," Devina said, "but I
think actually it is a case of 'fine feathers make fine
birds.' If I had been dressed in my own clothes I am
quite sure no-one on board would have noticed me."

"Then enjoy them while you're at the Castle,"
Nancy-May said, "and when you leave, take one or
two which you like best with you. I can easily buy
more for myself later."

"That's very sweet of you," Devina answered,
"but your mother has given me so much already."

Nancy-May gave a little exclamation.

"That reminds me," she said. "I wanted to give
you a present of my own. Jake changed a lot of money
for me yesterday, but when I asked him for some for
you he wouldn't give it to me."

"What do you mean by 'a lot of money'?" Devina asked.

"It was what he wanted for the journey," Nancy-May replied, "and he asked the Purser to change it into pounds because I can't go to a Bank and sign a cheque until I'm married."

"No, of course not," Devina agreed. Then she said:

"It seems rather greedy, as your mother has been generous, but her cheque is in dollars and I cannot go to a Bank until I hear from you. I may not have enough cash to pay my fare from the Castle to London."

She had really forgotten until this moment how very little she had left when she had walked up the steps of 550 Fifth Avenue and prayed that she might get the position which was advertised.

"I tell you what we'll do," Nancy-May said. "I'll write out a cheque for the present I wanted to give you, and you slip up to the Purser's Office and change it into English pounds."

"I hate to ask you for anything after you have been so kind," Devina said in embarrassment.

"Oh, shucks!" Nancy-May replied. "You've been so kind to me, you know you have! And I hope, Devina, we'll always be friends."

"Of course we will!"

Nancy-May went into the Sitting-Room and a moment later came back with a cheque in her hand.

When Devina looked at it she gasped.

Quickly reckoning the exchange, she calculated that Nancy-May had given her about a hundred pounds.

"I cannot take all this!" she exclaimed.

"Of course you can!" Nancy-May answered. "You know as well as I do that I've loads of money. There is too much fuss made about it anyway. Besides, you may need all of that at Milnthorpe Castle—you never know."

"I think that is unlikely," Devina said, "but as long as I am pretending to be you I might have to . . . tip the servants and . . . things like that."

"Then put on your clothes and go to the Purser's Office," Nancy-May advised.

She hesitated, then she added:

"Don't tell Jake."

Devina's lips tightened for a moment.

She had the feeling that Jake was taking over Nancy-May's fortune even before she was his wife.

Then aloud she said:

"I will say nothing but thank you. It is very, very kind of you, and I shall be praying all the time you are on your way to Scotland that you are really doing the right thing and will find all the happiness in the world."

"I'm sure of that," Nancy-May said. "All the same, I would like you to pray for me."

"I will," Devina promised.

She dressed hastily, then went to the Purser's Office as Nancy-May had suggested.

He seemed surprised to see her so early, and when she appeared he ignored a number of other passengers who were clamouring for his attention.

"What can I do for you, Miss Vanderholtz?" he asked.

"I would be so grateful if you would give me this money in pounds, shillings, and pence," Devina answered.

The Purser took the cheque and said:

"More cash? I hope you'll be careful, Miss Vanderholtz. We have thieves and robbers even in England. You're carrying a whole lot of lose money about with you."

Devina thought it wisest to say nothing, and he handed her, as she had anticipated, over one hundred pounds, which she put in her bag.

'I ought not to take it,' she thought.

Then she told herself that it would save her from having to make up her mind immediately whom she should go to when she left the Castle.

Perhaps it might be a good idea to look for employment in London now that she could afford to stay in a Lodging-House while she did so.

She certainly shrank from the idea of landing up on the door-step of her cousins or going to her great-aunt who lived at Cheltenham and was always ill and inevitably disagreeable.

"I must find work of some sort," Devina told herself.

She wondered what Galvin Thorpe would say if she asked him if she could help him with his book.

Then she told herself she was the last person he would want to employ, and what was more, she would never have the courage to do anything but run away from him once he had learnt the truth.

She went back to the cabin to find that Nancy-May was dressed and to her relief, there was no sign of Jake.

"You've got it all right?" Nancy-May asked.

"Yes, and I have no words in which to tell you how grateful I am for your generosity."

"Just as I can't begin to thank you," Nancy-May replied.

She paused, then said in a serious voice:

"I realise it's going to be uncomfortable for you when you have to tell them the truth at the Castle. It's something I should hate to have to do myself."

"What would you hate to do?" a voice asked.

Both girls jumped, for they had not heard Jake come into the Sitting-Room.

"I was thinking of Devina having to face the Dragons at Milnthorpe Castle all alone," Nancy-May said.

"She'll be all right," Jake answered. "After all, she's English, so they can all sit down and say how disgracefully the Americans behave and it's just what might have been expected."

He spoke spitefully, but Devina laughed.

"I do not think it will be a case of 'sitting down,'" she replied. "More likely I shall be shown the door!"

She paused before she said pleadingly:

"Send me a telegram as soon as you can. I do not wish to lie for longer than I have to."

"We will, I promise we will," Nancy-May said before Jake could speak.

He drew out his watch.

"Everyone'll be going ashore in ten minutes," he said. "We'd better get down to the lower deck, Nancy-May. I've got all your baggage there and had it labelled in my name."

"You think of everything!" Nancy-May said admiringly.

"All you've got to do is bring your jewel-case," Jake said. "Don't forget it."

"Oh, I forgot!" Nancy-May exclaimed.

"Forgot what?" he asked.

"That Devina'll need some jewellery to wear at the Castle."

"Well, there's no time to give it to her now," Jake said quickly. "Come on! We've got to get ashore and hire a carriage to take us to the station. We can't travel on the boat-train."

"No, of course not," Nancy-May agreed.

She flung her arms round Devina's neck.

"Good-bye, kind, sweet Devina," she said. "You've been a real friend, you know that, and I'll always be grateful."

"Take care of yourself," Devina said.

"I'll take care of her," Jake interposed. "Come on, Nancy-May!"

He pulled open the door and started off down the passage.

"Good-bye!" Nancy-May cried as she rushed after him.

Devina sat down on a chair as if her legs would no longer carry her.

They had gone!

She had let this happen, had done nothing to prevent it. Was she right or was she wrong?

The question seemed to ask itself over and over again in her mind as it had done all night.

Then Rose came in from the State-Room.

"Ze young—so impetuous!" she said. "Eet not *un bon mariage* for someone zo rich. Ze French arrange theengs better."

"They are very much in love," Devina said, as if she felt she must defend Nancy-May.

Rose made an expressive gesture with her hands.

"L'amour," she said, *"pour M'mselle, oui,* but for *Monsieur?"*

She shrugged her shoulders.

"What are you saying, Rose?" Devina asked. "Surely you are not insinuating that Mr. Staten is not in love with Miss Vanderholtz?"

"Mais certainement, with *M'mselle's millions. Quel homme* could be anything else?"

Rose's reply only added to Devina's disquiet, but there was no time to discuss it further and anyway she had no wish to do so.

The stewards arrived to collect the luggage from both State-Rooms and Devina put on the attractive cape which covered her silk gown and a very elegant and expensive hat which went with the whole outfit.

"Certainly no-one I knew in England would recognise me at this moment," she told her reflection in the mirror.

Then, picking up the hand-bag with Nancy-May's initials on it in gold, she walked slowly from the cabin to the deck.

The passengers were going ashore and she saw Galvin Thorpe talking to Lady Taylor.

"Ah, there you are, my child!" Lady Taylor remarked when Devina joined them. "I wanted to say good-bye and apologise again for being so helpless during the first part of the voyage."

"You were very kind and I was so grateful for all you did for me," Devina answered.

"Mr. Thorpe tells me that he is escorting you to Milnthorpe Castle," Lady Taylor said, "so I leave you in good hands. Actually, I'm not going to London."

"Then good-bye," Devina said, "and thank you very much indeed for everything!"

"I will write to your mother as soon as I have time," Lady Taylor promised. "And please give her my kind regards when you tell her you have arrived safely."

Devina smiled but could not bring herself to ut-

ter yet another lie by saying she would do what Lady
Taylor asked.

"I think we should go ashore," Galvin Thorpe
said, and Devina preceded him down the gangway
and onto the Quay.

It was raining but they had only a very short
walk before they were under cover and within sight of
the boat-train.

Only as they moved towards it, with a porter carrying their hand-luggage, did Galvin Thorpe say:

"I suppose Miss Castleton is with the Courier?"

"What Courier?" Devina asked.

"I thought he had made contact with you," Galvin
Thorpe replied. "He came to see me, and I told him
that I would be bringing you ashore and he should
see to the luggage."

"I expect that is . . . what he has . . . done," Devina said.

Then, drawing a deep breath, she added:

"As it happens, Miss Castleton received bad news
this morning."

"She did?"

Galvin Thorpe did not sound very interested. He
was looking towards the train, obviously searching for
the Courier.

"Yes, her . . . her m-mother is ill," Devina said,
"and as she was . . .very upset, I told . . . Mr. Staten
to see her safely into a tr-train which would take her
h-home."

"You mean the watch-dog has left you unpro-
tected?" Galvin Thorpe asked with a note of surprise
in his voice.

"I felt sure I would be quite . . . safe in England
. . . and with you," Devina answered.

She thought he looked surprised, but at that moment the Courier came forward.

He was an elderly man, obviously experienced in
making everything run smoothly.

Devina saw that the hand-luggage was already
arranged in a private compartment. The morning papers were on one seat with a large hamper and there

was a heated foot-rest and golden rugs lying tidily on two corner seats.

"Everything's on the train, Mr. Thorpe," the Courier said respectfully.

"Thank you," Galvin Thorpe replied. "Miss Vanderholtz, this is Mr. Moore, who has been at the Castle ever since I was a small boy. He used to take me back to school when the holidays were over."

Devina held out her hand.

"Thank you for looking after my luggage," she said with a smile.

"I have unfortunately been unable to find your companion, Miss Vanderholtz, or your detective."

"I have just been telling Mr. Thorpe that Miss Castleton received bad news this morning. Her mother is ill and I have sent Mr. Staten to accompany her home. I think they had to leave from a station in the town."

"Well, that would account for it," Mr. Moore said.

"Here is my lady's-maid," Devina said, glancing back to where Rose was following them, looking very French and very dismal in the rain.

"She's in the next compartment to you, Miss Vanderholtz," Mr. Moore said, "and I'm sure Mr. Thorpe's valet will look after her."

Devina thought that doubtless the company of a man would cheer Rose up, but she hoped Rose would not become too confidential. She felt quite certain that Galvin Thorpe's valet would repeat to his master anything that she told him.

She got into the carriage, Galvin Thorpe followed her, and Mr. Moore shut the train door behind them.

Devina looked with interest at the picnic basket, which was very large and bore a Ducal coronet.

"Are visitors to Milnthorpe Castle always so well looked after?" she enquired.

"I imagine so," Galvin Thorpe replied, "but, as you are well aware, you are a very special guest."

There was something in the way he spoke which made Devina's heart sink.

She hoped they were not going to fight the entire

journey. Then she told herself she could always shut her eyes and pretend to go to sleep.

She had to admit that Galvin Thorpe looked very distinguished and very English in his well-cut travelling-clothes. He had taken off his tweed cape and thrown it down on one of the empty seats.

"How long will it take us?" Devina asked.

"Only two hours," he replied, "but as I am quite certain you hurried through your breakfast, as people always do when they leave a ship, you will be glad in a little while to sample the delicacies which I am sure this hamper contains."

Devina put her feet on the hot foot-rest and covered her knees with a rug before she said:

"I have never travelled so comfortably before."

"I am sure your father's private railway-car is the very acme of comfort, and for all I know he may have a train of his own."

Too late Devina thought she should have remembered that people like the Vanderholtzes had their own carriages which were attached to a train. She believed, in fact, that there were private trains in America, even as there was the Royal Train in England.

She said nothing and Galvin Thorpe sat down opposite her. When he was comfortable he said:

"I suppose you realise that conventionally we should be travelling with a Chaperon. I feel sure Lady Taylor would be very shocked if she knew we were alone."

"I am sorry if you feel I am . . . compromising you," Devina answered.

She saw by the twinkle in his eye that he was only teasing, and he replied:

"Naturally I have to worry about my reputation, but as it happens I was thinking of yours."

"I could hardly . . . refuse to . . . allow Miss Castleton to go to her . . . mother."

"No, of course not, and I imagine, if the truth were known, you are glad to get rid of the watch-dog. A rather tiresome young man, who, I thought, presumed on his position and drank too much for someone in an official capacity."

Galvin Thorpe spoke with a note of authority in his voice which made him sound severe.

"Of course, you are American," he went on as if he were speaking to himself, "but I cannot imagine that a young English girl who is as important as you are would be allowed to cross the Atlantic with such a young companion and indeed such a young detective."

"I suppose no-one visualised anything terrible happening to me on a British ship," Devina replied.

"Thank you for the compliment to my country," Galvin Thorpe said, "but there are always unseen dangers for someone like yourself who is written up continually in the newspapers and surrounded by an aura of gold, which incites envy, hatred, and greed amongst those who have not got it."

"Perhaps whoever said: 'Love of money is the root of all evil' was right," Devina said.

"It is certainly responsible for a great deal of misery and violence in the hstory of mankind," Galvin Thorpe agreed. "That is why I thought my Dinka friends, who are quite content with their cows, beads, and reed skirts, are very much happier than any other race I have ever known."

"Tell me more about them," Devina asked.

He looked at her before saying:

"I have a feeling you are deliberately trying to change the subject from yourself."

"Why not?" Devina enquired. "I am tired of . . . myself. It is a subject I know . . . too well."

"Actually, it is one I find very interesting," he said. "As I have told you before, you are different from what I had expected."

She did not answer him and after a moment he went on:

"It is rather like opening a book being quite sure you know the story, but finding it very different and therefore completely enthralling."

There was a note in his voice which made Devina feel shy.

She looked out the window as, after a last-minute flurry of passengers and porters, the train began to move.

Devina had a glimpse of the *Mauretania* towering
above the Quay, her four funnels and two masts sil-
houetted against the grey sky, her superstructure very
"spick-and-span."

Galvin Thorpe followed the direction of her eyes.

"A very fine ship!" he said. "And once again the
British have won the battle of the Atlantic!"

"Was it a very fierce battle?"

"One that was bitterly fought by the Germans and
the Americans," he answered. "I suppose now they
will begin to build even bigger ships, and on it will go
again, with the British doubling the size of her rivals'
vessels."

"It was certainly very much more comfortable
than travelling in a small ship," Devina said. Then, remembering that she was not supposed to have left
America before, she quickly added: "At least, so I
have always been told."

"And rightly so," Galvin Thorpe said. "I once
sailed down the coast of Africa in a cargo-boat that
was not only extremely small but also unseaworthy, an
experience I hope never to repeat."

"Where were you going?" Devina asked eagerly.

She kept him talking about his adventures for
quite some time.

Then Galvin Thorpe insisted on opening the hamper and they discovered it contained pâte sandwiches
and delicious little pastries filled with different meats.

There was a bottle of champagne and for Galvin
Thorpe, if he preferred it, a flask of whisky, and
wrapped in flannel, enormous peaches which Galvin
Thorpe told Devina came from the hot-houses at the
Castle, and a bunch of muscat grapes which looked too
beautiful to eat.

There was a bottle of champagne and for Galvin
Thorpe, if he preferred it, a flask of whiskey, and
there was coffee, which he said jokingly was a conces-
sion to Devina's origin, for otherwise it would have
been tea.

"You are in England now," he said, "and you
must get yourself used to our national beverage."

"I thought that was beer," Devina replied, and
he laughed.

"Certainly at the Castle it flows in the Servants' Hall, but I am sure your French maid will turn her nose up at it and demand wine."

"Will she get it?" Devina asked curiously.

"The servants in great houses like my cousin's fare well if not better than their masters. I remember once I spent a very gloomy evening not with my cousin but with an aged nobleman who insisted on a monologue in which he repeated and rerepeated himself."

He laughed and continued:

"When I retired to bed I learnt from my valet that they had passed a very amusing evening in the Servants' Hall and danced afterwards. I thought then that I was on the wrong end of the stairs."

Devina was about to tell him something amusing that had happened to her father in somewhat similar circumstances, but just in time she remembered that she was supposed to be American.

She deliberately made two or three remarks pronouncing the words as Nancy-May would have done.

They finished eating, and Galvin Thorpe, lying back against his seat, said:

"Is your heart beating excitedly at the thought of what lies ahead?"

"I am looking forward to seeing Milnthorpe Castle," Devina replied.

"And its owner? Surely it will be intresting to meet a Duke—especially one you intend to marry?"

"I have told you before, Mr. Thorpe, I have no wish to . . . discuss such . . . things."

"But you must think about them, and I want you to think very carefully and very objectively about your marriage."

"I cannot . . . think why you should be . . . interested."

"I can give you a very good reason, but I do not intend to do so."

"Why not?"

"Because there would be no point. I have already told you what I think about you: that I believe you to be different from the type of American young woman who comes to England determined to strike a bargain."

He paused before he said:

"Are you really prepared to go on with this monstrous Exchange and Mart?"

She looked out the window, very conscious that his eyes were on her face.

"You are lovely in a way that I did not realise when I first saw you," he said quietly. "There is something ethereal about you, something which has deepened and grown more obvious every time I have seen you."

His voice died away. Then after a pause he said:

"I find myself not looking so much at your features but at the soul I can see in your eyes, at your spirit, which shines through your skin like a light! You were meant to inspire and guide a man, not degrade him by making him dependent upon you financially."

There was a note in his voice which made the blood rise in Devina's pale cheeks, and her hands fluttered as she looked towards him to say:

"Please . . . do not speak to me like that. You are taking . . . advantage of our being . . . alone."

"And why should I not take advantage of an opportunity which will never occur again?"

"Because it is . . . wrong."

"Wrong? What is wrong about it?" he enquired almost fiercely. "I am a man and you are a woman. But you are different from other women because you are sitting on a gold mountain, and that is supposed to put you out of reach of ordinary mortals like myself."

"Please . . ." Devina pleaded again.

"You shall hear what I have to say," he insisted, "while for the moment we are alone where no-one can interrupt us. It does not matter if you have sixpence in the Bank or six million. Just for this short while we are cut off from the world outside and you have to listen to me."

"I would . . . rather you did not . . . say it."

"But I intend to do so. I intend you to know what I feel about you."

Devina looked down at her hands.

"That is . . . very obvious."

"Is it? What do you think I feel?"

"What you felt when you first saw me," Devina answered, "was contempt and, I think too, disgust."

"Yes, I did feel that when I first saw you," Galvin Thorpe replied. "But afterwards, when I talked to you, something happened which has never happened to me before in the same way."

She glanced up at him for a moment and quickly looked away again.

"I fell in love!" he said in a deep voice.

"No . . . no!"

The words burst spontaneously from Devina's lips.

"It is true," he said quietly. "I fell in love and have found it impossible these last days at sea to think of anything but you. Your face and the vibrations coming from you seem somehow to be a part of me."

"But it is not true . . . you are . . . imagining this."

He smiled.

"I am much older than you and I assure you I know myself very well. What I feel for you is not just different but completely revolutionary compared with how I have ever felt before."

It was what Devina had felt too and she knew exactly what he was trying to say.

"I never imagined," Galvin Thorpe went on, "falling in love with a young girl, and certainly not an American. But nationalities are not of the least importance; what lies between us like a deep gulf is the difference in our circumstances."

"Y-you mean . . . money?" Devina said.

"Of course I mean money," he answered. "What man would willingly saddle himself with a woman who is encased with gold to the extent that he would feel it was impossible for her to be normal or have the ordinary feelings that another woman would have?"

"I do not . . . think that is . . . true."

"It is true," he contradicted, "and you know it! How could any relationship survive the knowledge that she was always the one who gave and he the one who took?"

He waited for her to speak, then went on:

"The man you marry will be labelled a fortune-hunter, a creature kept by the wealth of his wife! How could that do anything but sap his pride, his principles, and of course his self-confidence?"

Devina drew in her breath.

For one wild moment she thought she might tell him the truth, tell him that the woman he thought he loved possessed nothing in the whole world.

Then she told herself that she would not only be betraying Nancy-May, she would be deliberately asking him to condemn her for her part in the deception.

It would also make him embarrassed because he had declared himself in love with someone who in fact did not exist.

He was seeing her in a particular way because he believed she had money. Would he feel the same if he saw her without it, as a very ordinary English girl?

Perhaps, despite all he had said, it was the aura of importance, of wealth, that in fact had attracted him.

Perhaps not the actual thought of the millions lying in the Bank, but the luxury, the exquisite gowns, the whole frame which focussed attention on the occupant of it.

'I cannot tell him,' Devina thought.

She knew she was afraid of seeing the expression in his eyes change, of losing the deep note in his voice which moved her as she had never been moved before.

Because he had said he loved her she felt her whole body vibrate with a sudden wild elation.

It made her feel as if he carried her away into a magic land where, as he had said, there were only the two of them.

And yet, because his whole conception of her was based on a falsehood, she dared not tell him the truth.

Suddenly he bent forward towards her.

"Suppose," he said, "suppose I asked you to come away with me now, to forget that we are expected at the Castle, to forget the Duke is waiting for you—would you come?"

His voice sent little thrills running through her, and because she wanted so much to hear him go on talking in that deep, passionate voice, she said:

"If I was not . . . myself, if I was not as you say 'sitting on a mountain of gold,' then I would . . . listen to . . . you."

"And you would come away with me without any more palaver?"

"If I did . . . perhaps you would be . . . disappointed."

"Perhaps you would. Perhaps you would find the life without so many expensive comforts, without servants and diamonds, with only at times the sand to sleep on and a small tent over your head, a very poor exchange for feather beds and Aubusson carpets."

Almost despite herself Devina looked into his eyes and was unable to look away.

"I would give you the moon, the stars," he said, "and the far-off horizon which we would fight to reach, only to find there was another horizon further ahead. But I would love you and make you love me."

His voice deepened and he went on:

"We would feel that strange instinct within ourselves reaching out to each other, making us move in the same rhythm as we did when we were dancing."

"It . . . could be . . . very wonderful," Devina whispered.

"More wonderful than I can say in words," he said, "and you would come alive in a way you have never been alive before! But if you go on now to your Duke, you will never be alive again."

There was something fatal in the way he spoke, which made Devina feel as if she shivered.

Yet at the same time she tingled with the awareness that his eyes were still holding her captive and it was very hard to breathe.

"I love you!" he said very softly.

Then so abruptly that she felt almost as if he threw cold water over her, he said roughly, and his voice was raw:

"But my love, like the magic I have been offering you, is just a mirage. You are still sitting on your golden mountain, and I have not the right equipment with which to climb it and reach you."

He had broken the spell which held them.

Now they both looked blindly out the windows at the passing countryside, while Devina felt her heart pounding in her breast and her breath coming quickly between her parted lips.

They sat for a few minutes without speaking. Then Devina realised that the train was slowing down and they were drawing into a wayside station.

It was only a small station and she knew it was the type of Halt that people of great importance were allowed to erect on the main lines where trains could stop for them at their request.

As she realised this she saw written up: HALT FOR MILNTHORPE CASTLE.

"We are here!" Galvin Thorpe exclaimed.

She knew that he was as surprised as she was that the journey had passed so quickly.

The carriage door was opened and as they stepped out she saw a man waiting on the station.

As he walked towards them with a smile on his face, she knew from his bearing, and perhaps because he looked like what she had expected, that he was the Duke of Milnthorpe.

"Hello, Galvin!" he exclaimed when he was within a few feet of them. "I thought I would come and meet you."

"That was very kind of you, Robert. May I introduce you to Miss Nancy-May Vanderholtz?"

The Duke put out his hand, saying:

"How do you do? Let me welcome you to England."

He was pleasant-looking and rather younger than she had expected. He looked almost like an overgrown school-boy, or perhaps an Undergraduate.

"What do you think I have brought to meet you?" he asked eagerly.

"I have no idea," Devina replied.

"My new car! You are not afraid to go in a car, are you?"

"No, of course not."

"I expect Miss Vanderholtz has been in a number already," Galvin Thorpe remarked.

"Well, this is the most fabulous machine you could ever imagine, Galvin!" the Duke said. "Remember how the one I had last year always broke down? This is reliable! This is a real goer! I cannot wait for you to see it!"

"There is no reason why you should," Galvin Thorpe said with a smile.

"Then come on. Moore will look after the luggage," the Duke said impatiently.

He hurried ahead of them just like an excited school-boy, Devina thought. She and Galvin Thorpe followed more sedately.

Devina looked at him from under her eye-lashes.

'Galvin is a man,' she thought, 'a man compared to the Duke, and I love him! I love him with all my heart. But, oh, God, what can I do about it?'

Chapter Six

Although Devina had been in the stately Fiat landaulet which Mrs. Vanderholtz used for shopping in New York, there was something very exciting about travelling in the Mercedes which belonged to the Duke.

He fortunately kept a chiffon scarf in it for any female passenger to tie on her hat, for he drove at twenty miles an hour, which he told Devina was the speed limit in England.

"I can actually take her at fifty, and have done so in the Park," he boasted. "My old Napier could never go as fast as that without breaking down."

"You will scare the stags, if not the workers," Galvin Thorpe remarked from the back seat.

At the same time, Devina thought he was rather impressed with the Mercedes and the speed with which they reached the Castle.

This was even more imposing than she had imagined and in fact looked exceedingly beautiful when they first glimpsed it rising above huge oak trees in the Park.

The Duke's standard was flying on the roof and Devina could not help feeling that if Nancy-May had seen it she would have regretted giving up everything it entailed for Jake.

Then she told herself she must not be cynical and that love conquered all things.

'Except,' she thought, 'when a man cannot . . .

endure to have a wife with a great deal more . . . money
than he . . . has.'

She was still trembling inside with the emotions
that Galvin Thorpe had aroused in her and she wondered what he was thinking as they travelled on towards the Castle.

They crossed a bridge, drove into a gravelled
court-yard, and stopped in front of a long flight of
steps which led up to a heavily studded front door.

"There! What do you think of her?" the Duke exclaimed as he pulled on the brakes.

"I congratulate you, Robert," Galvin Thorpe said
before Devina could speak, "and you certainly drive a
great deal better than you did when you last endan-
gered my life!"

"You insult me!" the Duke said with a laugh.
"Even Mama admits that I am a very careful driver."

"I have a feeling your mother is prejudiced in your
favour," Galvin Thorpe said as he smiled.

They walked into a huge Hall which was hung
with stags'-heads and a profusion of ancient weapons
and flags captured in battle.

Devina, however, had no time to look about her,
for the Duke hurried across the Hall and opening a
door shouted:

"Mama—your guests are here!"

Devina followed him into a long Drawing-Room
with windows opening onto a terrace outside.

A woman rose from the side of the fireplace and
as she walked towards her Devina thought that the
Dowager Duchess looked exactly as a Duchess should.

She had white hair and thin aristocratic features,
and every inch of her proclaimed pride and breeding.

Her smile was welcoming and she held out a blue-
veined hand with almost a Royal grace.

"Welcome to England, Miss Vanderholtz!" she
said. "It is delightful to have you with us and I am
only so sorry that your dear mother could not accompany you."

"She was very sad about it when she broke her
leg," Devina answered.

The Duchess greeted Galvin Thorpe and he kissed her cheek. Then she asked:

"Where is your companion, Miss Vanderholtz, who I understood was with you?"

Again Devina told the story of Miss Castleton having to go to her ill mother.

Because she knew Galvin Thorpe was listening, she felt herself stammering and making it sound somehow unrealistic that she had asked her detective to accompany her companion.

So you and Miss Vanderholtz travelled alone!" the Duchess said to Galvin Thorpe with just a touch of reproof in her voice.

"It was only a journey of two hours," he answered dryly.

"Yes, yes, of course," the Duchess agreed, "and I do understand, Miss Vanderholtz, that there was nothing else you could do in the unfortunate circumstances."

Devina was taken up to her room, which she was sure was one of the largest and most important in the Castle, and when she came downstairs again they had luncheon.

After the meal was over the Duke wanted to take her driving in his car, but the Duchess insisted they should first visit the stables and the gardens, all of which Devina enjoyed.

When they returned there were some of the rooms in the Castle to see. The tour extended before and after tea, and almost before she was aware of it, it was time for dinner.

After they had visited the stables, Galvin Thorpe had disappeared, and Devina found herself thinking of him and longing for him and finding it hard to concentrate on what the Duchess was saying.

She gave the Duke little chance to speak, but he seemed used to being an attentive audience and was obviously prepared to let his mother dominate him as she obviously dominated the Castle and the estate.

'He is very young,' Devina thought. 'Far too young to be married.'

But she suspected that, apart from wanting a rich bride, the Duchess had also set her heart on having an heir to inherit the title.

The Duchess was very formal, and by the time she went to her own room to change, Devina was beginning to dread the moment when she must tell her that she was not who she appeared to be.

She was sure the Duchess would be furious that the show which was being put on to impress the heiress to the Vanderholtz millions had all been wasted.

There was a dinner-party with near neighbours, and although they only sat down twelve in the huge Baronial Dining-Room, everything was done on such a grand scale that Devina felt it was almost like a stage-set.

The footmen in knee-breeches and powdered wigs, the huge gold candelabra on the flower-decorated table, the long array of dishes served on gold plate, the procession in to dinner—all were things which she felt must seem theatrical except to those to whom it was an habitual occurrence.

She recognised that Mrs. Vanderholtz had tried to produce in New York the way of life that had been carried on for centuries at Milnthorpe Castle.

The imitation had not seemed genuine, while Devina knew that everything that happened at the Castle was steeped in tradition.

The guests had sat after dinner in an even larger and more impressive Drawing-Room than the one Devina had already seen.

They talked in pairs until on the stroke of eleven o'clock the most distinguished guest rose to her feet to say good-bye.

Devina had not during the evening had a chance to speak to Galvin Thorpe.

He had not been able to approach her after dinner when the Duchess had sat her down in a chair next to a distinguished-looking old gentleman who she learnt was the Lord Lieutenant.

After that she was moved round the guests, talking to each in turn according to their importance.

Before she reached Galvin Thorpe, however, it was time for bed.

At the bottom of the Grand Staircase a footman handed her a lighted candle in a gold candlestick, and she managed to say:

"Good-night, Mr. Thorpe, and thank you for bringing me . . . here today."

There was just a little throb in her voice as she remembered the way he had spoken to her in the train, and she felt sure he was thinking of it too.

He bowed and replied:

"It was a pleasure, Miss Vanderholtz."

His voice was cold and Devina felt despairingly that they were miles apart and that what he had called "the magic" between them would never come again.

Rose helped her to undress and chattered incessantly of the grandeur of the Castle and the large number of servants there were below-stairs.

"C'est magnifique, M'mselle!" she kept exclaiming. " 'Ow could *M'mselle* Nancy-May geeve up anything so beeg, so noble, for that unimportant detective?"

Rose spoke with a scorn in her voice which told Devina that she considered Jake Staten of no Social standing, and she herself was inclined to agree, although she was not prepared to say so.

"Let us hope she will be very happy, Rose," she remarked aloud.

"For me, thees would be 'appiness," Rose replied, "and I theenk *M'mselle* verry stupeed!"

Again Devina felt like saying she agreed with her, but she knew it would be a mistake. She got into bed.

When Rose had left she lay for a long time in the darkness, thinking first of Nancy-May, then recapturing the moment when she had looked into Galvin Thorpe's eyes and been unable to look away.

Over and over again she could hear his voice saying:

"I would give you the moon, the stars, and the far-off horizon which we would fight to reach, only to find there was another horizon further ahead."

That is where he would go when he left here,
she thought, and she would never see him again.

She could picture him moving away from her and
she wanted to hold out her arms and beg him to stay.

"I love . . . you!" she whispered in the darkness.

But she knew despairingly that once he knew the
truth, his love for her would die and she would never
find the magic of which he had spoken.

*   *   *

Devina awoke with a start to find that Rose was
pulling back the curtains.

"I wake you early, *M'mselle,*" she said. "A telegram arrive."

"A telegram?" Devina exclaimed, sitting up in
bed. "But surely they cannot have reached Scotland
so quickly?"

"That ees what I thought, *M'mselle,* so I bring eet
tout de suite. It is not yet seven o'clock."

She held the telegram out to Devina as she spoke,
and as she took it from her she waited by the bedside,
full of curiosity.

Devina opened the telegram.

For a moment as she looked at the signature she
thought there was some mistake and that it was not
intended for her. Then she read it through slowly.

> *Come quickly to the Park Hotel, Kensing-
> ton. I want you.*
>
> *May Flower*

Suddenly she understood, as Nancy-May had
known she would.

Nancy-May would not have been able to sign
her own name. But the *Mayflower* was the ship on
which Mrs. Vanderholtz's ancestors were supposed to
have crossed the Atlantic to a new life in America.

It was, Devina knew, a cry for help, and holding
out the telegram for Rose to read she leapt out of bed.

"We must go to her, Rose. We must go at once!
What can have happened? How could they have got
no farther than London?"

"You theenk this from *M'mselle* Vanderholtz?" Rose questioned.

"But of course it is! I understand why she has signed herself 'May Flower,' and she must be in terrible trouble. Oh, Rose, what can have happened?"

Although it was obvious that the Frenchwoman was reluctant to leave the comfort and grandeur of the Castle, Devina forced her to realise that they must do their duty.

Far quicker than she would have believed it possible, she was dressed, and with Rose following she hurried downstairs.

It was so early that the maid-servants in mobcaps were moving about the Hall and the footmen were in shirt sleeves.

They looked up in astonishment as Devina, wearing the silk cloak in which she had arrived and the same smart hat on her head, came down the stairs.

She was just about to ask for a carriage to take her to the station when a man walked in through the front door.

Her heart, leaping in her breast, told Devina who it was even before he looked at her in astonishment.

"Where are you going?" he asked. "What has happened?"

"I have received a telegram from a friend of my ... mother's, asking me to meet her in ... London today, because she is ... returning to America this ... evening."

Devina spoke quickly, giving the excuse she had made up while she was dressing.

Galvin Thorpe did not reply and she gabbled on:

"You will understand that if I do not hurry she will have left London before I can meet her. She may have thought I arrived earlier than I actually did, but it is very important, she says, that I should see her. So I feel sure Her Grace will understand."

"I am sure she will," Galvin Thorpe replied quietly.

"If I could just have a ... carriage brought round

to . . . convey me to the . . . station," Devina suggested hesitatingly.

"I will take you there," he said, "and I think it might be a good excuse for me to drive Robert's car. He is so proud of it that I feel I may not get another chance."

He smiled at her, then gave the order to a footman to tell the chauffeur to bring the car to the door.

As Devina stood nervously waiting, Galvin Thorpe came to her side to say:

"You look rather perturbed. Are you very fond of this friend of your mother's?"

"Yes . . . very!" Devina answered. "And I think she would be extremely . . . upset if I refused to do as she has asked."

"Then I will make your excuses to my aunt," Galvin Thorpe promised, "and tell her why you have had to rush away in this unexpected manner."

Devina started guiltily.

"I intended to . . . write a note," she said. "Please tell Her Grace that I do not mean to be impolite, it is just something I . . . have to do."

"I am sure she will understand," Galvin Thorpe said again soothingly.

It was actually a very short while, but to Devina it seemed a long time before the car came to the door.

Galvin Thorpe told the chauffeur that he intended to drive and Devina sat in the front beside him while the chauffeur and Rose sat behind.

He certainly drove as well as the Duke, if not better, and they reached the small station in what seemed an extraordinarily short time.

"I will find out what train you can catch," Galvin Thorpe said as soon as they arrived.

He disappeared into a small room where Devina guessed it was possible to communicate with the nearest station and also put up the signal outside the station itself.

Devina was looking down the line almost as if she would will the train to come quickly, not only because she was anxious to reach Nancy-May but because she was afraid of any intimate conversation between herself and Galvin Thorpe.

He might probe too deeply and she would be trapped into saying something which might make him suspicious.

He came walking towards her from the station building and she thought how handsome and at the same time how elegant he looked.

Hastily she looked away from him in case he should see not only her admiration but also a look of love in her eyes.

"You are in luck," he said. "You can catch the morning express, which is due in five minutes, and you will be in London soon after half-past-nine. At what time do you expect to return?"

"I do . . . not know," Devina replied vaguely.

"Send a telegram as soon as you do know," he said. "Then either Robert or I will meet you."

He paused before he said with a faint smile:

"You will not be popular if you are late for dinner. There is a special party arranged for you tonight."

"I will certainly . . . try not to be . . . late," Devina answered.

"Do you want me to tell you that you have made an excellent impression so far? My aunt is delighted both with your appearance and your manner. She kept saying to everyone last night that it was hard to believe you were really American!"

He laughed.

"I had better warn you that that is the sort of compliment you will have to get used to in this country, and I suspect that it will be said to you over and over again."

"I am quite sure most Americans would think it an . . . insult," Devina said.

"But you are intelligent enough to realise that it is not meant as one, and the greatest compliment any English person could pay would be to say that you were like them."

"No wonder you are looked upon as an arrogant race!" Devina replied.

Because she meant to be provocative she made the mistake of looking directly at him.

Then everything they were talking about, everything she was about to say, went out of her mind!

She could only stand there feeling that once again she was caught in a magic spell in which he swept her away towards an indefinable horizon.

They both started when there were the sounds of an approaching train and a few seconds later it puffed towards them and in what seemed a resentful manner came to a halt.

Galvin Thorpe assisted Devina into an empty First-Class compartment and Rose sat down opposite her. He closed the door, saying:

"Do not forget to let me know when you are returning." And without waiting for her to answer, he walked away.

Almost immediately the guard blew his whistle and waved his flag before swinging himself back into his van.

Devina did not look out the window to wave to Galvin Thorpe as she wanted to do.

'I should have thanked him,' she thought to herself.

She wondered how many more times she would be able to feel grateful to him for taking care of her.

She wondered what he would have said if she had asked him to come with her to London and to help Nancy-May, if she was in fact in trouble as she anticipated.

Then she told herself that if nothing was really wrong she would be returning to the Castle for perhaps one or two more days, before the whole masquerade came to an end and she would have to leave under a cloud of shame.

Devina knew that whatever the ultimate penalty, it would be worth it to see Galvin Thorpe.

She wanted to talk to him and to know those moments of strange magic when they looked into each other's eyes and the whole world and everything in it was lost except love.

Exactly on time, despite the delay, the train reached London.

Hurrying Rose through the crowds at the station, Devina found a hackney carriage and they were on their way to Kensington.

"Th' Park 'otel, Ma'am?" the cab-driver asked when Devina gave him the address. "Oi thinks Oi knows it."

As they turned into a small, quiet, tree-filled Square off the busy thoroughfare Devina found that the Hotel was in fact a modest one.

It must, she thought, originally have been a large house or perhaps two which had been commercialised when Kensington ceased to be residentially smart.

She had been thinking frantically as they drove from the station what she should say to Jake Staten to explain her arrival.

She was quite certain that he would not be aware that Nancy-May had sent her a telegram.

She also wondered under what name Nancy-May would be registered, as it was obvious that she would not use her own.

Devina paid the cab-man and with a bravery she was far from feeling walked into the Hall of the Hotel and up to the Registration-Desk.

She felt slightly more confident when a tired clerk looked at her in surprise and was obviously impressed by her appearance.

"I would like to engage a room for myself and one for my lady's-maid," Devina said.

"Certainly, Madam. You are fortunate in that one of our best rooms is available."

He turned the visitors' ledger round towards Devina as he spoke.

Picking up the pen slowly, she quickly scanned the names of the guests already inscribed on the page at which it was open.

She was so anxious that for a moment she found it difficult to read the various handwritings. Then she found what she sought: "Mr. J. Staten," and below his name: "Miss N. Staten."

In the column headed ADDRESSES was written: "New York," and, what was important, the clerk had entered the numbers of their respective rooms.

Jake Staten was in number 73. His supposed sister was in 74!

Devina wrote her name as "Mrs. Castle," then she asked:

"I wonder if it would be possible for me to have room seventy-five? I stayed here some years ago and remember that that was the room I occupied."

The clerk looked at a plan of the Hotel which he had in front of him.

"Again you are fortunate, Madam," he said. "Number seventy-five is available and there is a room on the other side of the corridor which would be suitable for your lady's-maid."

There was a pause, then he asked:

"Is your luggage, Madam, outside in a carriage?"

"It is coming later from the station," Devina replied. "There was too much for us to bring it with us."

"It will be sent up to you, Madam, immediately it arrives," the clerk said.

He took two keys from a board on the wall just behind him, and bowing respectfully led the way to the stairs.

Devina felt as they climbed them that everything was going more smoothly than she had dared to hope.

She was only afraid that they might meet Jake Staten on the stairs before she and Rose could get to their bed-rooms.

But they were lucky and reached the first floor without seeing anyone, and the corridor along which they walked was also empty.

The clerk opened a door, then entered first to hurry across the room and pull back the heavy fringed curtains.

"Please ring, Madam, for anything you require," he said.

"I will, and thank you."

He bowed, showed Rose to her room on the other side of the corridor, opened the door for her, then left them alone.

"Listen, Rose," Devina said in a low voice. "Miss Vanderholtz is next door and Mr. Staten is in the room beyond. What we have to discover is if they are in the Hotel at this moment."

" 'Ow we do that?" Rose asked.

"I suppose by knocking on the door. But then, if Mr. Staten is with Miss Nancy-May, he will know of our arrival."

They both thought for a moment, then Rose said:

"You leave it to me, *M'mselle,* I ring for *la femme de chambre* an' ask her many question. I know *cettes femmes,* they always ready t' talk."

"Could you do that, Rose?"

"Leave to me, *M'mselle.*"

Rose left her, and Devina, taking off her silk travelling-cloak and her hat, went to the window.

Because the Hotel was built in the Georgian style there was a small balcony made with elaborate wrought-iron outside each window.

Unfortunately, they did not connect with each other, and although Devina stood at the end of her balcony and tried to look in through the window of Nancy-May's room it was impossible to see anything but lace curtains.

It seemed to her that Rose was gone for a long time, and when she came back Devina knew by the expression on her face that she had found out what they wanted to know.

"That Jake Staten go out," she said, "just before we arrive."

"Alone?" Devina asked quickly.

"Alone, *M'mselle.*"

"Oh, Rose, thank you! That is what I wanted to hear!"

Devina slipped out of her own room and knocked on the door of number 74.

At first there was no reply and she knocked again.

"Nancy-May!" she called in a low voice. "It is I . . . Devina!"

As she spoke she looked up and down the corridor in case she should be overheard, but there was no-one about.

She heard a movement on the other side of the door, then Nancy-May's voice said:

"Is that—you, Devina?"

"Yes. Open the door!"

"I can't! I'm locked in!"

"Locked in?" Devina repeated incredulously.

"Yes. Jake locked me in and took away the key."

Devina drew in her breath.

She thought at first she would go downstairs and demand that the door be opened, as she was certain that the management would have a master-key.

Then she thought this would certainly cause a commotion, and if there was a row it might reveal Nancy-May's identity.

"Devina—are you still there?" Nancy-May asked from behind the door. "Oh, help me, Devina! Please help me!"

"I will," Devina said firmly. "Do not worry, Nancy-May."

She went back into her own room, followed by Rose.

"What are you going to do, *M'mselle?*"

"I am going to get into *Mademoiselle*'s bed-room by the window," Devina said.

Rose gave a little cry.

"C'est impossible! C'est dangereux! Non, non, M'mselle, you might keel yourself."

"Listen, Rose, you keep watch," Devina said. "If you see Jake Staten coming up the stairs, come and knock on the door. Otherwise, listen in case I call you to help me."

Rose started to protest but Devina went determinedly to the window.

She went out onto the balcony and looked at the distance between it and the one outside Nancy-May's window.

There was in fact a gap between them of less than three feet. At the same time, if she fell she would fall into the basement, and even if she was not killed it would certainly result in considerable injury.

"I have jumped much greater distances than that!" Devina told herself.

Trying to keep calm, she climbed up on her own balcony, holding on with one hand to the wall of the house. With the other she lifted her silk skirt and her lace-trimmed petticoats.

Then, taking a deep breath and praying not to be afraid, she put her foot on the top bar of her own balcony and jumped!

She landed in the centre of Nancy-May's balcony, and apart from grazing her hand as she put it out to support herself she was quite unhurt.

Then Nancy-May had the window open and was crying:

"Oh, Devina. How could you do that for me?"

She had her arms round her and was holding on to her almost frantically.

Devina gently led her back into the bed-room.

"I am here," she said. "Now tell me what has been happening."

Nancy-May burst into tears.

"I've been so miserable—so frightened," she said, sobbing. "I thought you wouldn't come. Oh, Devina, take me away!"

Devina sat on the side of the bed and pulled Nancy-May down beside her.

She was dressed only in a lace-trimmed chemise, her corset, and her petticoats.

For a moment Nancy-May could only weep, then Devina said quietly:

"I know Jake is out for the moment, but he may return. We must be quick if we are to do anything."

"I don't want to marry him!" Nancy-May cried. "He frightens me, Devina—and you are right when you say he only wants my—money!"

"What makes you think that?" Devina asked.

"It was the way he—behaved after we set off in the train and . . ."

There was a pause, then Nancy-May said in a very small voice:

"And the way he—kissed me."

Devina put her arms round her again and Nancy-May went on:

"He—hurt me, and when I was—frightened he said I was not to make a fuss."

"Did you tell him you had changed your mind about marrying him?"

"I—I was not sure at first that I had changed it —completely," Nancy-May said, "but suddenly I didn't want to go away to Scotland with him. That was after he discovered when we got to London that the express to Glasgow had already left!"

"So you had to stay the night," Devina said.

"Yes," Nancy-May answered, "but then . . ."

She hesitated.

"Then what?" Devina prompted.

"He—wanted me to pretend I was his—wife so that we could have one—room in the Hotel."

There was no doubt from the way she spoke that Nancy-May had been shocked and afraid.

Devina held her a little closer as she went on in a low voice:

"Wh-when I told Jake I would not do that because it'd be—wrong, and we couldn't share a—room until we were married,—he said: 'If you're playing fast and loose with me I'll give you a baby, then you'll have to marry me!"

Nancy-May gave a little cry and the tears were pouring down her cheeks again.

"I—it was the way he—said it, Devina, which told me that he didn't really—love me and—only wanted my m-money."

"He is despicable!" Devina said sharply. "But now we have to get you out of here. Perhaps I ought to ring for a maid."

"No—no!" Nancy-May said. "Take me away without Jake knowing. I—can't face him—I can't— listen to the things he'll say to me. I'm frightened! Devina—I'm frightened of him!"

"I do not think you could jump as I did," Devina said. "You might fall, and that would be awful!"

"I can't do that anyway," Nancy-May answered. "Jake has—taken my clothes away—they're in his room."

Devina drew in her breath.

She knew now that she had saved Nancy-May from a man who was definitely a crook.

Already she was beginning to realise how cleverly he had planned the whole thing—perhaps alone, perhaps with an assistant whose brains were sharper than his.

"It will be all right," she said. "I will call Rose and I am sure she will find a chamber-maid who will open the door for us."

She jumped off the bed, hurried to the window, and stepped out onto the balcony.

"Rose!" she called. "Rose!"

The lace curtains draped across the windows of her room moved and she thought it was Rose coming in response to her call.

"Hurry!" she said urgently.

Then onto the balcony stepped not Rose but Galvin Thorpe!

*   *   *

Travelling back in the train to the Castle, Nancy-May sat beside Devina and held on tightly to her hand.

With her tear-stained face and her unhappy, depressed manner she was very different from the vivacious girl who had captivated so many young men aboard the *Mauretania*.

Galvin Thorpe had been, Devina told herself, more kind and gentle with her than she had imagined it would be possible for any man to be.

He had taken command from the first moment he had appeared, and she had never been so thankful for anything in her life as the fact that he was there.

As they stood facing each other she had stared at him wide-eyed, hardly believing it possible that he had materialised like a genie in a fairy-story just when she wanted him most.

"I felt you might need my assistance," he said, "so I got into your train just before it left the station."

"And you followed me here?" Devina asked.

He nodded and she said:

"Then . . . please . . . we   must   get   Nancy-May away at once!"

He smiled.

"That is who I imagined was next door," he said. "Is she locked in?"

Devina nodded.

"Leave everything to me," he said, and disappeared through the lace curtains.

Devina waited, then she called Rose.

"*Monsieur* Thorpe ees 'ere," the Frenchwoman said as though Devina did not know. "That ees good! Now he deal with Jake Staten!"

"I am sure he will," Devina replied. "Will you please give me my cloak?"

Rose looked surprised but she fetched it, and Devina, taking it from her without further explanation, went back to Nancy-May, who was still sitting disconsolately on the bed.

"Everything is all right, dearest," she said. "Mr. Thorpe is here and will cope with everything."

"M-Mr.—Thorpe?" Nancy-May asked almost in horror. "B-but he must not—know who I am."

"He knows already," Devina replied. "Anyway, forget all the secrets and the pretence. They were all thought out by Jake Staten, and the sooner we get away the better!"

"He won't let me go—I know he won't let me go!" Nancy-May cried, clinging to her in a sudden terror.

Devina thought that a man who could reduce anyone so happy and light-hearted as Nancy-May to such a state deserved to be shot, but aloud she said:

"There is no reason to be frightened of him any more. We all make mistakes, and everyone will forgive you when they realise he was only a crook who was imposing upon you."

She kissed Nancy-May's cheek before she continued:

"Anyway, how could you be expected to recognise those sort of people on sight? They are too clever. That is why they succeed in their crookedness."

Nancy-May would not, however, be comforted.

Only when finally Galvin Thorpe had the door open and walked in to announce that they all were leaving immediately did her eyes seem to light up for a moment.

"She must have something to wear," Devina said before she could speak. "He has taken her clothes away."

She saw by the expression on Galvin Thorpe's face what he thought of Jake Staten, but he said nothing.

He simply arranged to get the door of the next room opened and Rose appeared a few moments later not only with one of Nancy-May's gowns but also her jewel-case.

Quickly, while Galvin Thorpe waited in the corridor, Devina and Rose dressed Nancy-May, then when they joined him Devina said:

"What about the rest of her things?"

"She can afford to lose them," Galvin Thorpe said sharply. "We do not want a scene if that man returns."

Devina realised that as well as the fact that he was determined to prevent anything happening which might find its way into the newspapers.

Incredibly quickly he had them all packed into a closed carriage and they drove off to the Grosvenor Hotel.

There they had a quick meal before they caught a train which would take them back to Milnthorpe Castle.

Nancy-May was too depressed to eat very much, but Devina, having had no breakfast, was hungry.

Rose, sitting at another table and supplied with half a bottle of French wine, was delighted with the whole drama through which they had passed.

"I think you should make sure that she does not tell the other servants at the Castle what has occurred," Devina said in a low voice.

"I have thought of that," Galvin Thorpe said. "I will go and talk to her while you have a cup of coffee."

What he said Devina did not know, but she had a

suspicion that he promised Rose a reward if she kept her mouth shut and was quite certain that as the Frenchwoman loved money she would keep the secret.

Now, with Galvin Thorpe opposite her in the railway-carriage, Devina could understand why he was successful in his explorations and in any adventures he encountered on his travels.

There was something forceful and at the same time persuasive about him.

She felt that everyone else like herself would trust him in an emergency to do what was right and know that the outcome of anything he undertook would be successful.

"I love him!" she whispered in her heart.

Then she remembered that the blow she had feared had fallen and now he knew the part she had played in this regrettable incident which might have ruined Nancy-May's life.

'He will blame me,' Devina thought, 'because I should have stopped it from the very beginning. I should have refused to take any part in the pretence.'

It was humiliating to think that she too had been deceived by Jake Staten into thinking that he really loved Nancy-May for herself, and that a girl who was too immature and too inexperienced to know her own mind should really be allowed to sacrifice everything for love.

'I have been a fool!' Devina thought humbly. 'And in a way it is all my fault. I should have wire-lessed the Vanderholtzes from the ship and told them what was happening, then left everything in their hands.'

Because she felt so ashamed of herself and her stupidity she could not meet Galvin Thorpe's eyes and she was certain there would be only condemnation in them.

Instead she concentrated on trying to make Nancy-May more cheerful and less apprehensive of the consequences of her actions.

"I don't want to—go to the Castle," she said when they had been travelling for a little while. "I want to go home—but how can I—face Poppa and Momma?"

"I think," Galvin Thorpe said before Devina could speak, "that it would be a mistake to upset them at this moment. They are too far away to do anything effective and will feel helpless and frustrated."

He let Nancy-May digest this before he went on:

"Besides, we three are all agreed, I think, that the one thing that must never happen is for anyone to say anything that might make the Press think there is a story somewhere. You know how they ferret things out if they are on to even the suspicion of a scent."

"I would never be able to go—anywhere or see —anyone if that—happened," Nancy-May said in misery.

"That is why we must prevent it," Galvin Thorpe said firmly. "And quite frankly, I think cables flashing backwards and forwards across the Atlantic are dangerous!"

"B-but what will the Dowager Duchess and the —Duke think?" Nancy-May asked.

"You can leave them to me," Galvin Thorpe answered.

He thought for a moment, then he said:

"Well, actually I will leave the Duke to you."

Devina looked at him in surprise, and was even more surprised when the Duke met them when they arrived at Milnthorpe Halt.

"I got your telegram, Galvin," he said, "and as you said it was important that I should meet you, here I am!"

"It *is* important!" Galvin Thorpe said. "And we will tell you all about it as soon as we are clear of the station."

The Duke looked mystified, and even more so when his cousin did not introduce the newcomer.

There was a carriage for Rose, and getting into the car they drove about a mile away from the station.

"Stop under these trees!" Galvin Thorpe ordered. "We have a tale to tell, as the Bards used to say."

Obediently the Duke pulled up, and when they

were in the shade of the trees and out of the hot afternoon sun he turned round in the driving-seat.

"What is happening?" he asked. "I feel it is something sensational, Galvin. I know that expression of
yours of old!"

"It is something very sensational and exciting,"
Galvin Thorpe replied.

He bent forward from the back seat as he spoke,
and Devina, who was sitting beside him, thought he
infused a certain magic of his own into everything he
did and everything he said.

She had not been surprised when as they had got
into the car he had assisted Nancy-May into the front
seat, which, for her, as Miss Vanderholtz, was her
rightful place.

She now felt a little quiver of excitement go
through her because Galvin Thorpe was so close to her.

Now he said to the Duke:

"We need your help, Robert, on something very
important that concerns Nancy-May Vanderholtz."

The Duke automatically looked at Devina, and
Galvin Thorpe said, touching Nancy-May on the
shoulder:

"This is Miss Vanderholtz, the guest you were
expecting yesterday, and the lady beside me, who took
her place last night, is in fact English and her name
is Devina Castleton."

The Duke looked astonished, then he said eagerly:

"I say, what is going on? Do tell me about it."

Galvin Thorpe told him the story, accentuating
the fact that Nancy-May had been the victim of an
unscrupulous, clever, and experienced crook.

He made it appear that she had been forced really
against her will to elope with him but had had the
good sense to realise his hypnotic influence over her
the very moment they left Southampton.

He even told how she had sent Devina a telegram
and signed it "May Flower."

"By Jove, that was clever!" the Duke said admiringly. "How did you manage to send it off without
that man being aware of it?"

"I—I wrote it when he was doing something else," Nancy-May said, "and although he's taken all my money, I found I had half a sovereign in my bag which I had won playing a gambling-game on board ship."

"That was lucky!"

"Yes, wasn't it?" she said. "So when the chamber-maid came to undo my gown, I slipped it into her hand with the telegram and begged her in a whisper to send it off at once. I was terrified that Jake, who was in the next room, would hear what I was saying."

"That was brilliant of you!" the Duke exclaimed. "You must have felt you were taking part in a detective-story."

"It was—very frightening," Nancy-May said with a little sob in her voice.

"I am sure it was. But nobody could have been as brave as you. I think you behaved splendidly!"

He went on saying admiring things all the way back to the Castle and Devina saw that Nancy-May was reviving like a wilting flower.

In fact as they drove down the drive and the Duke offered to teach her how to drive his car, she looked almost like her former self.

"Will you really do that?" she cried. "How wonderful! Can I have my first lesson now?"

"Tomorrow," Galvin Thorpe said firmly before the Duke could reply. "We have to see the Duchess before we do anything else."

It was extremely difficult to tell the sorry tale to the Duchess.

Galvin Thorpe had seen her first alone and prepared her for what she was to hear, and she listened to Nancy-May without saying a great deal, but Devina felt she noticed that the Duke took every opportunity of championing Nancy-May and saying how sporting she had been.

Finally, when there was no more to tell, the Duchess said coldly:

"I can only say that it is extremely unfortunate that this should have happened, and that the part played by both you young women is, to say the least

of it, reprehensible! But there is no time to discuss it
any further, otherwise you will be late for dinner."

She rose from the sofa on which she was sitting
to say:

"You had better all go and change and leave it
to me to put things in their proper perspective."

Devina felt as if they had all been dismissed by
the Headmistress. But as they climbed the stairs Nancy-May whispered irrepressibly:

"What a perfectly gorgeous house! Do you think
I've lost all chance of owning it?"

Chapter Seven

Devina was dressed early, helped into her gown rather hurriedly by a house-maid who had other duties to attend to.

Rose of course was in attendance on Nancy-May.

Looking at her reflection in the mirror, Devina thought that this was perhaps the last time she would wear one of the beautiful gowns that belong to Nancy-May.

It had been fascinating to see the difference expensive clothes made to her appearance.

She wondered frantically if tonight Galvin Thorpe would admire her as he obviously had before, or if he would look at her only with condemnation because of the way she had behaved.

She wondered how it could be possible to speak to him alone, if only for a few seconds.

Now she wished that she had not been so embarrassed and shy on the train journey which had made her unable to seek some reassurance that everything between them was not finished.

'I love him!' she thought miserably. 'But he will never love me again.'

She was quite certain that one of the bases of love was trust.

Just as she trusted him completely and absolutely, it would be impossible for him ever again to trust her, knowing how much she had lied and deceived him.

She was just about to go to Nancy-May's room
and see if she was ready for dinner when there was a
knock on the door.

"Come in!" Devina called.

When it opened, the Duchess's lady's-maid came
into the room.

"Her Grace would like a word with you, Miss."

"Now?" Devina enquired.

"Her Grace'll see you in her *Boudoir*. If you're
ready, I'll take you."

"I am ready," Devina answered.

She picked up her handkerchief and followed the
maid along a wide corridor which she knew led to the
South Wing of the Castle, where the Dowager Duchess
had her apartments.

She realised as soon as they entered through dou-
ble doors that the rooms in the South Wing were larger
and more beautifully furnished than any in the other
part of the Castle.

She knew this was where the reigning Duke and
Duchess would sleep, and she wondered if in fact these
rooms would ever belong to Nancy-May.

There was, however, little time for speculation,
for the lady's-maid showed her into a *Boudoir* that
was redolent with the fragrance of hot-house flowers.

It was furnished exquisitely with French furniture
and pictures which made Devina long to inspect them.

But the Duchess was waiting and the look on her
face commanded all her attention.

Wearing a grey satin gown with long ropes of
priceless pearls round her neck and a diamond tiara
on her white hair, the Dowager Duchess was not only
extremely impressive but rather awe-inspiring.

As soon as the maid had closed the door behind
her she said:

"I sent for you, Miss Castleton, because I have
been thinking of the predicament in which Miss Vanderholtz finds herself."

"I am exceedingly . . . sorry about . . . it," Devina
said in a low voice.

"And so you should be!" the Duchess retorted.
"I cannot exonerate you for not communicating with

your employers the moment you were aware of the way this crook had inveigled a very young girl into his clutches."

"I . . . realise now I was very . . . much at . . . fault."

"Recriminations do no good," the Duchess said sharply, "but I hope another time you will behave with more responsibility and certainly more common sense."

"I will certainly try to do so, Your Grace," Devina said humbly.

"My immediate concern at the moment," the Duchess went on, "is Miss Vanderholtz's position as my guest. No-one, as you are well aware, must know what has occurred, and I think the first thing that is important is that you should not be seen in her company."

Devina looked up in surprise as the Duchess continued:

"The only real difficulty, as far as I can see, are the guests who met you last night at dinner."

The Duchess paused for a moment before she said:

"Fortunately, they are all elderly and it is my experience that people see what they want to see."

"You mean . . ." Devina began, trying to follow the Duchess's reasoning.

"I mean," she said, "that when they meet Miss Vanderholtz again it is doubtful if they will suspect her of not being the person they met last night."

"Oh, I understand what Your Grace . . . means."

"I thought you would. Therefore, tonight, Miss Castleton, you will dine upstairs and it would be best for everyone if you left early tomorrow morning."

Devina did not reply and she said:

"I expect you wish to go to London, and a carriage will take you to catch the same train that you took this morning."

"Yes . . . I would like to go to . . . London," Devina murmured.

"Then that is settled! I presume Mrs. Vanderholtz paid you for your services? But if you are short of money—"

"No, no!" Devina interrupted. "I have been paid very generously and require nothing more."

"Then I will say good-bye, Miss Castleton, and hope you manage to find suitable employment in the future."

"Thank you."

The Duchess obviously did not intend to shake hands, but moved away to show that the interview was at an end, and Devina walked towards the door.

As she reached it the Duchess said:

"I shall of course be obliged to inform Mrs. Vanderholtz of your part in this conspiracy, but I hope it will not prejudice your future in any way."

"I shall not be applying to Mrs. Vanderholtz for a reference, Your Grace."

Devina walked in what she hoped was a dignified way from the room, closing the door quietly behind her.

The Duchess's lady's-maid was waiting outside to open the door into the corridor.

"Thank you," Devina said and went back to her own bed-room.

As she reached it she told herself that it was exactly what she might have expected to happen and what she should, if she had had any sense, have suggested herself.

She knew her thoughts had been so preoccupied with Galvin Thorpe, and she had longed so desperately to spend another evening in his company, that she had been blind to what ought to have been her proper behaviour in the circumstances.

She should in fact not have returned to the Castle at all.

When they had reached the Halt and left the train she should have insisted on waiting for another back to London.

Nancy-May, and perhaps even Galvin Thorpe, might have protested, but it was still the way she should have behaved, rather than put herself in the position of being turned out of the Castle like a badly behaved kitchen-maid without a reference.

The Duchess had not insulted her, she had merely behaved as she would have done herself, with common sense and in the best interests of Nancy-May.

But Devina could not help thinking how annoyed her father would have been that she had allowed herself to get into such an unfortunate position.

'I will just have to forget all about it,' she thought.

But she knew the real question throbbing inside her was whether she would also have to forget Galvin Thorpe.

The first thing she had to do, however, was to find her own clothes and get them ready to leave with her tomorrow morning.

She must also say good-bye to Nancy-May.

Hurriedly she went along to her bed-room, only to find that she had already gone downstairs and there was only Rose tidying away her things.

"I am leaving first thing tomorrow morning, Rose," Devina said. "Will you show me where you have put my clothes?"

"I pack in one of ze trunks, *M'mselle*," Rose replied. "I weel tell a footman to take downstairs so they weel be ready when you leave."

"That would be very kind," Devina said.

"Also some gowns in trunk *M'mselle* tell me on ze shep you wear she not want again."

"She did say something about my having some of her clothes," Devina answered, "but I would rather not take them."

"La la! You glad when you away from 'ere," Rose said practically. "I've no time unpack."

"I am sure you are tired. It has been a long day," Devina said. "At the same time . . ."

"Not worry, *M'mselle*," Rose said. *"M'mselle* verry lucky have you look after 'er. If you not save 'er she marry t' that *sale cochon.*"

"That is true."

"Then forget trunk," Rose advised, "and hurry, *très vite,* or you late for dinner."

"I am dining upstairs," Devina answered.

Without waiting to answer the questions she was

sure Rose would want to ask, she went back to her own room.

She had only just reached it when there was a knock on the door.

A footman informed her that her dinner was waiting for her in an adjacent Sitting-Room which Devina had not seen before.

It was a small room, part of a Suite with bed-rooms on either side of it. However, it had obviously not been intended for use, for there were no flowers such as filled the Duchess's *Boudoir*.

The dinner was small but delicious. Devina, how-ever, had to force herself to eat, telling herself this might be the last expensive meal she would eat for a long time.

She sipped the wine which the footman poured out for her, and when she had finished dinner she carried a cup of coffee back to her bed-room.

She sat down in front of the dressing-table, telling herself to be sensible: she must forget the past and make plans for the future.

It was hard to think how the attractive, exquisite-ly dressed girl who faced her in the mirror could earn her own living.

"What talents have I that are saleable?" Devina asked herself, and knew the answer only too well.

There were only two possible careers open to im-poverished gentlefolk: to be a Governess to small chil-dren or a companion to some cantankerous old lady.

She decided that to be a Governess was prefer-able, and yet she wondered if she was too young to establish such employment and perhaps, although it sounded conceited, too pretty.

She remembered that her own Governesses had always been rather nondescript women of indetermi-nate age.

Devina thought that most ladies would hardly want a very young woman in the house with whom perhaps they would be compared to their disadvantage.

Devina suddenly felt very depressed. The future looked black and the present more so.

How could she leave the Castle without saying

good-bye to Galvin Thorpe? Would he get in touch with her? And anyway, it would be almost impossible for him to do so.

She felt sure he was not the sort of person who would compromise her by asking her to meet him outside in the garden when everybody else had gone to bed.

What was more, she had the uncomfortable feeling that the Duchess would deliberately not tell him that she was being sent away.

"He will surely be curious when I do not go down to dinner," she murmured.

Then she thought he might think she was tired and had deliberately chosen to rest after such a long and emotional day.

She contemplated writing him a note telling him at least where a letter could reach her . . . but would he wish to write?

Then she knew she could not humiliate herself by running after him. Besides, how could she bear him to answer such a note if it was only out of pity?

Then it struck her that if she did write he might imagine she needed financial help! Her whole being shrank in horror at such an idea.

"It is over! It is finished!" she said aloud. "As he said himself, the magic is only a . . . mirage. How could I expect it to be . . . anything else?"

After she had sat for a long time thinking, she undressed but was too restless to get into bed.

Instead, she walked about the room, looking out the windows at the stars overhead, before finally she sat down in a deep arm-chair, finding that every train of thought brought her back to one person—Galvin Thorpe.

"I love him!" she told herself, "and I shall never love another man in the same way."

She thought that perhaps anyone who heard her would laugh cynically at such an assertion at her age.

But she told herself that if she had an instinct, as he believed she had, then she was well aware that this was the love that came only once in a lifetime.

She envisaged herself getting older and lonelier

as the years went by, finding that her heart, once given, could never be given again.

It was too depressing to contemplate, and yet it was there, and she told herself that the dreams and the fantasies were over and she had to face reality.

She was still sitting in the chair, growing a little cold because the night air was cool, when the door opened and Nancy-May came tip-toeing into the room.

She looked towards the bed, then saw Devina sitting in the chair.

"Devina!" she exclaimed. "I was afraid you would be asleep. I asked the Duchess what had happened to you and she said in a most repressive tone:

" 'I will tell you of Miss Castleton's plans tomorrow. Please do not speak of her to anyone!' "

Nancy-May flung herself down on the floor at Devina's feet and said:

"What was she talking about? What has happened?"

"She very sensibly wants me to leave without anybody else seeing me," Devina answered.

Nancy-May looked at her enquiringly and Devina said:

"It is the right solution. You must not tell anybody that I was on the ship with you, and eventually everyone, even you, will forget there was ever such a person as Devina Castleton."

"I understand what the Duchess is trying to do," Nancy-May said slowly. "At the same time, I can't bear to lose you. You're my friend, the best friend I've ever had!"

"Perhaps when everything has blown over and everyone, including you, has forgotten that Jake Staten ever existed, then we can meet again," Devina said.

"Yes, of course. We'll do that!" Nancy-May agreed.

She put her head on one side and with a mischievous expression in her eyes said:

"If I marry the Duke you can come and stay here."

"Are you thinking of doing so?"

"He's certainly amusing," Nancy-May replied,

"and he likes the same things as I do. Tomorrow I'm going to see his stables and I've bet him a hundred dollars I'll beat him in a steeple-chase."

"I heard your father say what a good rider you were when you were on his Ranch in Arizona."

"I'll beat the Duke! Or perhaps it'd be better, as Englishmen like to be dominant, to let him win."

"It is certainly an idea," Devina smiled.

"He's nice," Nancy-May said reflectively, "and I never imagined anything could be so magnificent as the Castle!"

Devina thought there was no doubt there would be a happy ending to Nancy-May's story.

When finally the American girl said good-night she unfastened a star-shaped brooch she was wearing on her gown and said:

"I want to give you this as a keep-sake."

"It is sweet of you, Nancy-May, but I cannot take anything more from you," Devina said. "You were kind enough to give me one hundred pounds, and I am keeping that so that I will have a chance to find some employment, and if I earn enough I shall pay you back."

"How can you be so horrid, so unkind?" Nancy-May asked angrily.

Devina looked at her in surprise, and Nancy-May said:

"I want to give you things. I love you. You helped me as no-one else has ever helped me before. And now you're becoming stuck up with pride."

Devina capitulated.

"Then I will not be, and thank you, dearest, for your lovely present and for all your kindness to me."

"I hate you to go away. I hate to lose you," Nancy-May said, "but I suppose we've got to do what the Duchess wants."

"Yes, we have no other choice."

Nancy-May flung her arms round her again and kissed her.

"Promise me we'll always be friends and that you'll write to me. I shall want to know exactly what you're doing, and I'll tell you about me!"

"I have a feeling I shall read about you in the newspapers," Devina said.

"If it wasn't for you it might have been a very different story," Nancy-May said, "and I'd never have been able to hold my head up again!"

"Forget it," Devina replied. "Forget everything except that you are going to be very happy."

Nancy-May gave a little sigh, then looked at the clock on the mantelpiece.

"Goodness!" she said. "It's awfully late. I'd better get some sleep or Robert'll think I look hideous in the morning."

She saw the question in Devina's eyes and explained:

"He asked me at dinner not to call him 'Duke.' He says it makes him feel old and pompous, and anyway he thinks Nancy-May is a lovely name and Vanderholtz too much of a mouthful."

Devina smiled and Nancy-May added:

"You know, one thing, Devina, being on the *Mauretania* taught me how to flirt, and I've come to the conclusion that I'm quite good at it!"

She gave Devina another of her mischievous smiles, then the door shut behind her.

Because she could not help it Devina was laughing when at last she got into bed.

*   *   *

Devina had asked Rose to have her called at six-thirty the following morning, and when a maid entered to pull back the curtains she felt that her eyes were heavy, as if she had only just dropped off to sleep.

She washed and started to dress, then realised that her own travelling-clothes were in the trunk which Rose had refused to unpack.

There was nothing for her to do but put on the same elegant and very expensive gown with its silk cape which she had worn the day before and the hat trimmed with flowers which matched it.

Devina thought it would be an exceedingly unsuitable garb in which to visit a Domestic Bureau as she intended to do as soon as she reached London.

'I must find lodgings first,' she thought, 'other-wise they will certainly mistake me for an employer rather than an employee.'

She was wondering, having tipped the maid who waited on her, how she could find a quiet, respectable place to stay in London.

She had actually left her bed-room before it oc-curred to her to wonder if the carriage which the Duch-ess had ordered for her would be at the front door or perhaps at a side-entrance.

After all, she was not leaving the Castle as an honoured guest, but as an employee whose services were no longer required.

Going back into her bed-room to ask the maid, she found that she too had no idea of the answer.

Devina therefore walked down the front stairs, telling herself that as it was so early there would be no-one about except the servants and doubtless one of the footmen could tell her what she wished to know.

She found, however, that waiting for her at the bot-tom of the stairs was the Butler, dressed correctly, and this morning, because she was obviously expected, there were no mob-capped maids to be seen and no foot-men in shirt-sleeves.

"Everything's ready for you, Miss," the Butler said, "and you've a pleasant day for travelling."

"Yes, indeed," Devina answered.

She felt almost surprised that the sun should be shining when she was feeling so low and depressed.

Yesterday she had found Galvin Thorpe in the Hall. Today she was creeping away while he was still asleep and she could not even say good-bye to him.

And yet, she asked herself, as the Butler went ahead of her towards the front door, had she any wish for anything different? What could they say to each other? And how could he utter banalities when once he had said he would give her the moon and the stars?

She walked through the front door and onto the steps, then below her she saw the Duke's Mercedes.

She was surprised!

Then a second later her heart started to beat

frantically, thumping so tumultuously in her breast that she found it almost impossible to descend the steps towards it.

The engine was running and the driver who was sitting at the wheel turned to watch her coming towards him.

The Butler helped her into the front seat.

"Good-bye, Miss. I hopes you have a pleasant journey."

"Thank . . . you," Devina managed to say in a voice which sounded curiously unlike her own.

The car started off and Galvin Thorpe drove down the drive in silence.

Only when they reached the main road and Devina had with trembling fingers managed to tie over her hat the chiffon veil which had been lying beside her on the seat did he say:

"You are looking very lovely this morning but still a little tired!"

Whatever Devina had expected to hear, it was certainly not this, and the tone of his voice only increased the tumult within her.

Her throat was constricted and it was impossible to speak.

"Are you really intent on going to London?" he asked after she had been unable to reply to his remark.

"I . . . I have to . . . go there," she forced herself to say. "I . . . have to . . seek employment."

"That is already arranged."

She turned round to look at him in sheer surprise, but his eyes were on the road in front.

"Wh-what do you . . . mean . . . 'arranged'?"

"I thought you could help me with my book."

"I . . . I would love to do that," she said, "but I feel . . . perhaps I might not prove a . . . competent secretary."

"Who said anything about you being a secretary?"

Devina could only stare at his profile, thinking she could not have heard him aright.

They were passing a wood and now unexpectedly Galvin Thorpe turned the car off the main road and up a cart-track which led into the wood itself.

He drove for about fifty yards to where the trees were thick on either side of them, drew the car to a standstill, and turned off the engine.

Slowly and without haste he turned to look at Devina, who was still staring at him in bewilderment.

"Now," he said, "can we talk about ourselves? You have been concerned long enough with other people's troubles and difficulties."

Because she was shy Devina could not meet his eyes.

At the same time, she was aware that something wild, warm, and exciting was moving inside her from her breast into her throat, sweeping away her fears and her depression as if the sun had come out and the night had gone.

"Look at me."

It was an order.

Slowly, because she was still a little afraid of what she might see, Devina obeyed him, and her eyes met his. She thought they looked into each other's heart.

Then with his face near to hers Galvin said:

"I love you and now there are no barriers to prevent me from telling you so."

Devina drew in her breath.

"Y-you know . . . nothing about m-me."

Galvin smiled.

"Have you forgotten I am an explorer? And let me tell you, my darling, I can imagine nothing more exciting than to use my expert knowledge to explore you."

Devina was trembling, not with fear but excitement. She clasped her fingers together as she asked:

"Have . . . you forgiven . . . me?"

"Not really," he answered, "and I want you to tell me how sorry you are."

He put out his hands towards her as he spoke and added:

"I think you will find it easier to do so without a veil and your hat."

He took them both off, then he put his arms round Devina and drew her close to him.

She felt she should protest and say many things

before she allowed him to kiss her, which she knew
he was about to do.

But she wanted so desperately, with her whole
being, to feel the touch of his lips on hers that she
could only surrender herself and feel that he made her
his captive.

The trees whirled round her, and his kiss, as he
promised, took her into a magic land where they were
together and nothing and nobody else in the whole
world mattered.

His arms tightened as he drew her closer and still
closer to him.

After what might have been a century he raised
his head to look down at her face. Then he was kissing her again, kissing her eyes, her cheeks, her chin,
and lastly her lips. . . .

When at last she could speak Devina made a little
sound which came from the very depths of her heart.

"I love . . . you!" she said, and her voice seemed
to break on the words.

"That is what I want you to say," Galvin replied.
"And now tell me that you are sorry you made me
not only very unhappy but unsure of myself for the
first time in my life."

"D-did I do . . . that?"

"What else could you expect?" he asked. "I loved
you almost from the first moment I saw you, but I
thought it was utterly impossible that you could ever
belong to me."

"You did not . . . want someone with . . . money?"
Devina murmured. "For I have nothing . . . nothing at
. . . all!"

"You have everything in the whole world which
matters."

His lips moved over the softness of her cheeks before he went on:

"It is not only your beauty, my precious, which
is worth more than all the gold in America; it is the
mysteries that lie deep in your eyes, and your vibrations which draw mine and tell me that you were
meant for me since the beginning of time."

"That is what I . . . feel about . . . you," Devina

said, "and when I thought . . . I would never see you again I knew I could . . . never love . . . anyone else."

"You never will! You are mine completely and absolutely, and I will never let you go."

"That is . . . what I . . . want, and I have been so . . . afraid of being . . . alone and having to . . . work for my . . . living."

Galvin smiled.

"You will have to work very hard for me," he said, "and perhaps, my sweet, it is a good thing that you are not afraid of discomfort. An explorer's wife has to put up with living in very strange and peculiar places. She certainly does not always travel in Mercedes cars or in Ocean Palaces!"

Devina turned her face against his shoulder.

"I do not mind how I . . . travel as . . . long as I am with . . . you."

"You will find mules and camels very unreliable," Galvin said. "Canoes have a way of upsetting one amongst the crocodiles, and dhows become becalmed whenever one is in a hurry!"

He was teasing but Devina answered almost passionately:

"I shall . . . love it! Love every . . . moment of . . . it, as long as you are there!"

"You can be sure of that," he replied. "And now tell me you are sorry you lied to me, which, incidentally, is something you will never do again."

"Never . . . never!" Devina promised. "But how could I have . . . told you the . . . truth without being . . . disloyal to Nancy-May?"

"I think your sense of loyalty is rather confused," Galvin said, "and I shall have to explain to you, my precious one, that it lies only with me and you are not to consider anyone else in any circumstances."

"Do you think I would . . . want to?" Devina asked.

He kissed her again, a long and lingering kiss. Then he began:

"Before I take you to stay with my mother . . ."

"Stay with your mother?" Devina interrupted, wide-eyed.

"We have to stay somewhere until we are married."

She hid her face against him and asked:

"Are you . . . really going to . . . m-marry me?"

"I have every intention of doing so," he replied. "But perhaps I should ask you first. Will you marry me, my adorable, lovely, if deceitful, Devina?"

She raised her head.

"You will not tell . . . your mother the way I . . . behaved?"

"I intend to tell no-one," he answered. "The Duchess is right. We must just behave as if the Miss Castleton I met in disguise on board the *Mauretania* never existed. We therefore start again from scratch."

Devina gave a sigh of relief.

"That is what I longed for . . . but how did you know I was leaving the Castle?"

"My valet told me he had heard it from Rose," Galvin replied. "It is hard work trying to keep a secret in a house full of servants."

Devina put her head against his shoulder.

"I thought . . . I would never see you . . . again," she whispered.

"You could never hide yourself away from me," he answered positively. "And now suppose you tell me who you are?"

Devina laughed.

"It seems impossible that we have done so much and said so much and yet you know nothing about me."

"I have already told you I know everything that matters," he said, "and perhaps I should add that I find your lips irresistible!"

He kissed her with a passion which brought a flush to her cheeks and made her feel breathless and a little shy.

Then with an effort, because it was hard to move back from the miraculous to the mundane, she said:

"My father was in the Grenadier Guards. I longed to talk to you about him when I saw you were wearing the Brigade tie."

"Your father was not George Castleton?" Galvin asked.

"Yes, but he died a year ago," Devina answered, "and that was why I went out to America, to look after my aunt who was ill."

"I knew your father," Galvin said, "and he was in fact very kind to me when I first joined the Guards Club as a young Subaltern."

"Papa was kind to everybody."

"Then I think he would be glad that I intend to be kind to his daughter."

Devina looked up at him.

"Please . . . be kind to . . . me," she pleaded. "Please . . . because I love you so much!"

"That is what I want to hear you say over and over again. In fact you cannot say it too often."

He kissed her again before he said:

"As I want you to meet my mother as soon as possible, I suppose we should be moving on. You have told me all I wanted to know, and she will welcome you with open arms when she learns that Colonel Castleton was your father. She always told me that she thought he was the best-looking man in the whole Brigade of Guards!"

"And I think . . . you are the best-looking man in the whole . . . world!"

"I believe in my mother's eyes I am a runner-up to your father, so you two should have a lot in common," Galvin said with a smile.

He began to take his arms away from her, then suddenly he pulled her almost roughly to him again.

"I love you! I love you until it is an agony and an ecstasy to know that my independence is at an end and I am caught and captivated as I have never been before."

"Do . . . you mean . . . ?" Devina tried to ask.

But he was kissing her, kissing her wildly, passionately, until it was impossible to breathe, impossible to think, but only to feel that she was enveloped by a magic which grew more intense and more wonderful every time he touched her.

"You go to my head, Devina!" he said, and his voice was unsteady. "Put on your hat and cover your face as much as possible with that veil; otherwise we will never reach my mother's house, and Robert will be furious if he does not get his car back this afternoon."

"How do you . . . intend to . . . return it?"

She tried to ask the question sensibly, but her eyes were shining like stars and her voice trembled because she had been so moved by his kisses.

"The chauffeur is already on his way with my valet and your luggage," Galvin replied carelessly.

Then, looking at her, he asked:

"How can you be so absurdly beautiful? What is it about you that seems to tug at my heart and give me a thousand sensations I have never known before?"

"Do I do . . . that?"

"You know you do!"

"It is the magic . . . the magic you . . told me might be a . . . mirage."

"That is something it will never be," he said positively. "Our magic will remain with us, my darling, to deepen and intensify all the years we are here on earth."

"That is . . . what I . . . want," Devina cried. "Oh, Galvin . . . I do . . . love you!"

"Say it again!" he ordered masterfully. "Say it again and again so that I can be really sure that you mean it and are not deceiving me."

"I mean it," she said, "I love you with . . . all my heart . . . with all my . . . mind, and with all my . . . body."

She blushed a little at the last word.

Then he was kissing her, fiercely, insistently, demandingly, and she surrendered herself to the irresistible magic of his lips.

ABOUT THE AUTHOR

BARBARA CARTLAND, the world's most famous romantic novelist, who is also an historian, playwright,
lecturer, political speaker and television personality,
has now written over 200 books. She has also had
many historical works published and has written four
autobiographies as well as the biographies of her
mother and that of her brother Ronald Cartland, who
was the first Member of Parliament to be killed in the
last war. This book has a preface by Sir Winston
Churchill. Barbara Cartland has sold 80 million books
over the world, more than half of these in the U.S.A.
She broke the world record in 1975 by writing twenty
books, and her own record in 1976 with twenty-one. In
private life, Barbara Cartland, who is a Dame of the
Order of St. John of Jerusalem, has fought for better
conditions and salaries for Midwives and Nurses. As
President of the Royal College of Midwives (Hert-
fordshire Branch), she has been invested with the first
Badge of Office ever given in Great Britain, which was
subscribed to by the Midwives themselves. She has
also championed the cause for old people and founded
the first Romany Gypsy Camp in the world. Barbara
Cartland is deeply interested in Vitamin Therapy and
is President of the British National Association for
Health.